the
WAITER

the WAITER

MATIAS FALDBAKKEN

SCOUT PRESS

New York   London   Toronto   Sydney   New Delhi

Scout Press
An Imprint of Simon & Schuster, Inc.
1230 Avenue of the Americas
New York, NY 10020

Originally published in Norway in 2017 by Oktober as *The Hills*

Published by agreement with Salomonsson Agency

Translated by Alice Menzies

First Scout Press hardcover edition October 2018

SCOUT PRESS and colophon are registered trademarks of Simon & Schuster, Inc.

For information about special discounts for bulk purchases, please contact Simon & Schuster Special Sales at 1-866-506-1949 or business@simonandschuster.com.

The Simon & Schuster Speakers Bureau can bring authors to your live event. For more information, or to book an event, contact the Simon & Schuster Speakers Bureau at 1-866-248-3049 or visit our website at www.simonspeakers.com.

Interior design by Bryden Spevak

Manufactured in the United States of America

10   9   8   7   6   5   4   3   2   1

Library of Congress Cataloging-in-Publication Data is available.

ISBN 978-1-5011-9752-9
ISBN 978-1-5011-9754-3 (ebook)

To Ida

PART I

A scared dog never gets fat.

—Norwegian proverb

THE PIG

THE HILLS, THE RESTAURANT, DATES FROM A TIME when pigs were pigs and swine were swine, the Maître d' likes to say—in other words from the mid-1800s. I stand here, straight-backed, in my waiter's uniform, and could just as easily have stood like this a hundred years ago or more. Extreme actions are carried out by grown people every day, but not by me.

I wait. I please. I move around the room taking orders, pouring, and clearing away. At The Hills, people can gorge themselves in surroundings which are rich in tradition. They should feel welcome, but not so comfortable that they forget where they are. With a few notable exceptions—some of the diners use the place like their own parlor. The Pig, one of our regulars, apropos of pigs, sits at table ten, by the window, at half past one every weekday. He tends to be punctual, but it's now 1:41 and he hasn't made an appearance. I do a loop of the entrance: no Pig. The cloakroom attendant, Pedersen, looks up from his paper. Pedersen is distinguished; as they say, he's seemingly seen it all. The guests trade their possessions—jackets, coats, bags, umbrellas—for a tag which they later, accompanied by a coin or two, swap for the same possessions when they leave. He has carried out these transactions with measured feeling and pride all these years; he does his job well. We're all diligent here at The Hills. It's a diligent place. Diligence and concern go hand in hand, I'm convinced of that.

Lunch is under way, and the main room has filled up with the upper middle class: silky skinned, softly spoken. Elegant clothes. There is a row of smaller café tables with classic marble tops by the entrance. In that area, the acoustics are sharper. Deeper into the room, tablecloths have been draped over the tables. There is clinking, but the noise is muted. Cutlery is moved around porcelain and up to mouths. Teeth chew, throats rise and fall, they swallow. It's all about eating in here, and I'm a facilitator. I never take part in the eating myself. I observe the intake. There's a considerable distance between the experience of ingesting a strong *picodon de chèvre*—the gastronomic explosion in your mouth—and watching the lips of someone else doing it. I set the tables as densely as possible, continental-style. There's not quite room, but I find space and squeeze in extra glasses, side plates, another bottle. It feels rich.

The chandelier isn't especially big, no bigger than a horse's nose bag, but it is heavy and hangs like a crystal sack from the low vaulted ceiling above the round table in the middle of the room. There are concentric circles of well-trampled mosaic tiles on the floor. All the woodwork is solid, dark, and worn. The two large mirrors are impressive. The reflective coating on the back of the glass has cracked here and there; it adds a nice patina. The art nouveau–esque oak frames around the mirrors were mounted in 1901. That's what the Bar Manager told me, elaborating with details about how the wood was dragged down from Ekeberg by Frits Thaulow's very own horse. The Bar Manager is the restaurant's memory; her face is like an academic's, but she's a bit too cheerful to be an academic. She sees everything.

The Hills might resemble a Viennese coffeehouse, but this isn't Vienna. It may look like a Grand European, but it's too worn, too grimy to match the grandeur you would find on the Continent. The establishment, the premises, has been called The Hills for almost 150 years now. The name comes from the Hill family, who ran an outfitter's shop there from 1846. The Bar Manager knows all about that. Benjamin Hill, the head of the family, a legendary but tragic dandy, originally from Windsor in England, gambled away two-thirds of the family fortune and stumbled into a painful bankruptcy which ended in attempted suicide and subsequent disability. The entrepreneur who took over the space opened a restaurant called La Grenade, but the original stained glass sign covering parts of the facade was so lavish and elaborate, not to mention well mounted, that he left it there, and the place became, as one can imagine, known popularly as The Hills. Benjamin Hill's energetic son eventually bought back the premises, took over the business, and resurrected the family name. The Hills remains under family control to this day.

From a curved brass pipe installed above the entrance, there are two thick curtains, which stop the heat from leaking out, each with calfskin sewed onto the edge to prevent wear and tear. In through this covering—The Hills's portal, or stage curtain, if you like—enters the Pig at last, smiling and nodding. It's almost ten to two—on the verge of the tolerable, that is. I neither nod nor smile back. I'm fundamentally neither a smiler nor a nodder. I don't have to make much of an effort to fulfill that particular waiter's instruction: a blank but obliging face to the guests. A poker face is all part of the craft.

"Apologies for the lateness," the Pig says, laughing apologetically, not with a grunt but with some kind of neigh. What do you call the neigh an ass makes? A bray? The Pig chuckles with a sharp bray, the way he often does. I've sometimes thought that the Pig is an ass, in the figurative sense; like an ass from European mythology and literature—not the ancient Greek "stubborn and stupid" ass, but the biblical "reliable and loyal" kind. Not that he's all that reliable right now.

"How many today?"

"Four, myself included," says the Pig.

"And the others are on their way?"

"I expect so."

There are many ways to dress. The Pig has chosen the only acceptable one: impeccably. He constantly has new suits, and, judging by the cut, the seams, and the quality of the material, they must be from the tailors on Savile Row or thereabouts. With an age of just over three score years, and dressed in such a wardrobe on a daily basis, he is in every sense an elegant man and model guest. The Pig fits The Hills like a glove. That's why we give him wiggle room with the number of guests, late arrivals, nonsense about the table, and so on. Not that it happens often. The Pig is wealthy—that much is clear—but he is also some kind of introvert. Steadily, quietly, he brings new contacts and acquaintances to The Hills, primarily for lunch, occasionally for dinner, always polite, and always with this impeccability in attire and manners.

"We've held the usual window table," I say, holding out my hand as I grab four menus and lead him through the room. With perfect timing, I pull out his chair and repeat the set phrase: "Some mineral water while you wait?"

"Yes, please."

He turns around and allows me to gently push the chair into the hollows of his knees. The Pig has a thick, grayish-white mane which he keeps short with a weekly trim. He turned gray during his twenties, while he was making a career in Paris, and was given the nickname Le Gris, which immediately became Grisen—the Pig—on his return to Norway. His eyebrows are still dark, giving him an intelligent look, like a Castelli, or doglike, like a Scorsese.

BLAISE

OLD JOHANSEN, THE HOUSE PIANIST, IS SITTING AT the grand piano on the mezzanine, looking at the vaulted ceiling and, to the left, into thin air. His stubby, Popelike fingers dance over the keys with light steps and considerable experience, producing seamless, barely audible music. Is this *Tafelmusik*? He chooses the great composers, Johansen, but it's still *Tafel*. Occasionally his eyes close as the notes trill in all directions, down into the restaurant. Old, stuffed Johansen. His head drops towards his shoulders, and it looks like he's nodded off for a moment, but then it rolls back into position and his eyes snap open. He carries on like that for hours. For a generation and a half now, he's been there, for endless stretches at a time, his head bobbing away, every day, on the mezzanine, that mid-ceiling, playing pleasant tones in succession for the guests. Since we arrive at different times, we rarely speak, but people say he has a sharp sense of humor.

The napkins are stacked with neat folds on a low shelf between two pillars in the middle of the room. A glass screen with pale art nouveau lines stands on top of the shelf, acting as a buffer between tables twelve and eight. If I find myself empty-handed, I often go over to the napkin shelf, where I hide behind the screen and straighten the napkins with an extra crease. The newbie, Vanessa, is a bit careless here. I make sure that The Hills's logo is in the top right-hand corner.

"Do you have the white burgundy today?" says the Pig.

"Of course."

I wait two tasteful beats before I ask the next question, to which I already know the answer.

"By the glass, or are we having a bottle?"

The Pig considers it.

"Listen, let's take a bottle."

Suddenly he gets up; I barely manage to pull out the chair for him. He extends his hands to a handsome couple approaching between the tables.

"Blaise [pronounced *Blés*]!" the Pig says enthusiastically. And then, with affection: "Katharina."

Blaise Engelbert is Katharina's husband; Katharina is Blaise's wife. They socialize with the Pig quite often, particularly Blaise. Blaise and his wife have married the mature versions of one another, the Bar Manager likes to say; the "old" version might be unfair to say, she says. After their respective detours around Oslo society—whatever that might be—they found one another and each is now, the Bar Manager further informs me, the oldest person the other has ever been with.

Katharina is first, and puts one foot before the other so that her maintained figure of forty-three to forty-five years is driven with determination in the direction of the Pig. Blaise is right behind, with another seven years on top of hers, wearing a gray suit with attractive stitching on par with the Pig's, possibly a notch above. Blaise has an excellent tie around his neck and a spring in his step. "Finesse"—the word always hangs in the air around this man. I tiptoe behind them, pull out their chairs, and have it confirmed that they would both like water and wine poured into their glasses.

The menu looks French and is delicately typeset in a softly spaced Bodoni. These are some of the words which appear on its two densely printed pages: "crackling," "plaice," "kid," "blue cheese," "cumin," "profiterole," "Jerusalem artichoke," "tart," "bouillabaisse," "squid," "roe," "date," "brisket," "rillettes," and "minke." To all this and more, the customers can point and have it prepared, with knowledge and flair, by the chef and his helpers before I or Vanessa, for example, bring out the dishes and the guests raise it to their mouths bit by bit. Truffles are also available. The truffle is key.

Vanessa, the freshman waitress with a tender appearance and a short, boyish hairstyle, with a talent hampered by ambition, straightens the tablecloths while I do a lap of the room, topping up a glass here and pleasing there. The poor actor who was recently convicted of forgery gets a refill; he's already starting to go slack-eyed. After the Pig's company has looked at the menu for a minute or two, I'm there pouring them water. Blaise brusquely rejects the white burgundy before I even have time to ask. He takes several large gulps of water, and I immediately refill his glass. Then he gives the sign that I can pour the wine. I turn the bottle clockwise after each pour, to catch the last drop. Tactfully, I lean over the Pig's shoulder and gently ask whether we are waiting for a fourth and final person. The Pig looks at his watch.

"Has anyone heard from her? It's 2:03. We're half an hour over." Blaise and his wife shake their heads.

"She did confirm?" Blaise says.

"Of course," says the Pig. "Absolutely."

The back of Blaise's head is oblong and youthful. He cranes his neck and peers towards the entrance. His hairline is classic and clean and favorably mirrors his jawline. The angle of his nose and brow and the curve of his cheekbones are also repeated with pleasing rhythm by his hairline as it runs from his temple down to his ear. His neck is boyish despite his age, his eyes alert. The collar of his shirt sits a comfortable six to seven millimeters away from the skin of his neck, in a beautiful fold. Blaise is fit but not overdone; he's sharp but not severe. Katharina and the Pig lean forward when he speaks, almost at a whisper. Blaise's voice is unusual. Where you might expect an ambitious pressure—as so often with handsome, almost pompous men—he produces a firm, authoritative but friendly, even verging on sensual voice.

"Would you like to wait awhile longer?" I say without seeming pushy.

The Pig checks the time again as Blaise raises his left arm to shake out his watch. It turns out to be an impressive A. Lange & Söhne; it couldn't be a Grand Lange I, could it? There's a hint of the braggadocio in Blaise.

"You can take the orders now, and the latecomer can . . . ," the Pig says, signaling, first with one hand and then with the other, that she can order when she arrives. I turn my attention to Blaise's wife to indicate that she can begin. Katharina chooses a mixed salad with Monte Enebro goat cheese, nuts, seeds, and passion fruit vinaigrette.

"Could I have extra nuts and seeds?" she asks.

"Extra nuts and seeds," I say.

Blaise changes his mind twice before he plumps for the creamy orzo with shallots. It's obvious that his indecision grates slightly on the Pig—obvious to me, not to the Engelberts. I turn to the Pig. It's his turn. He takes his time.

"The brown Valdres trout," he says.

"Yes?"

"What kind of crispbread comes on the side?"

"We have a crispbread from Hemsedal."

"Right."

"We have a wonderful sour cream dip to go with it," I say with a hooked index finger pointing downwards to illustrate "dip." What am I doing?

"Thanks, but no. No dip for me. I'll try the trout."

"Wonderful."

THE WALLS

ALONG THE WAINSCOTING WHICH RUNS BENEATH all the portraits, drawings, and paintings here at The Hills, a number of stickers have been stuck over the years. We allow it. That's the way it's always been. The sticking has died down somewhat now, but the odd new sticker still appears from time to time. It's not clear how the sticking began, but there are rumors that some avant-gardists who frequented the place during the 1920s did it to play pranks on a rich man who had his regular table at the other end of the room. What these jokes consisted of is difficult to see through today's optics, but down by the skirting board there are old, yellowed fragments of newspaper cuttings about this financier, Mr. Grosch. The avant-gardists cut out thin columns from the papers and glued them to the wall, often horizontally, at the very bottom; these were gestures to Mr. Grosch, gestures of spite. The crude clippings later crept upwards from the skirting boards and were followed during the '30s and '40s by flyers and small pamphlets, manifestos, primarily political material, before being covered over by commercial stickers during the '60s and '70s, old STP and Gulf images to begin with, then Castrol and RFI, followed by football teams and rowing clubs and so on, resulting in the conglomerate which now covers the wainscoting. If you took a cross-section of the paneling, you could carry out an archaeology of it, from early bohemian life to sport and trade; from the oldest, crustiest layers, which are golden brown and look almost like parchment, to the outer, fresher stickers. The wainscoting itself, small glimpses of which can be seen between the layers of stickers, is dark and matte, nearly as black as the ceiling above the hob in the kitchen. It's almost like a void between the marks. It's difficult to see where the stickers end and the wainscoting begins, where The Hills begins or ends, depending on whether you consider a wall to be the beginning or the end of a room, a locale, an establishment. Europe has certainly seen better days. One could claim that Europe's best idea was the Grand European.

Above the wainscoting, paintings, drawings, and the odd collage are crammed tightly together on the—and I apologize for this—diarrhea-brown walls with their coat upon coat of shiny beige paint—or is it lacquer? The art has "accumulated" over the years, meaning that it's impossible to describe The Hills's collection as anything other than *considerable* in a national context. There's a Revold hanging on one wall, a Per Krohg, and even a small Oda Krohg sketch by table five. Back in the '90s there was a lot of talk about conservation and the climate inside The Hills, but the

family has always taken a hard line, insisting that the pictures donated to the restaurant should remain there. It's easier now, after the
smoking ban, but some of the older material is fairly snuff colored.

A small, pre-cubist Braque oil landscape hangs above table
six, believe it or not. There's also a first-rate Léger in chalk by
the screen. The simple Schwitters collage framed in hideous teak
to the right, above the bar, was donated by Schwitters himself
when he was en route from Hjertøya to the capital in '34 or '35.
Gunnar S. has two handsome graphic prints at one end of the
room, plus one beneath the mezzanine. Large and small works
are hung side by side, all mixed up. There has never been any talk
of "re-hanging" the works here at The Hills; more is just hung.
They're still hanging more. Contemporary art is squeezed into
the gaps between older works. It's old and new, clean and grimy,
side by side. The quality varies considerably. A fifteen-by-twenty
coal sketch from the hand of Anders Svor hangs frame-to-frame
with an early Polaroid by Ed Ruscha and an atypical Cosima von
Bonin frottage. A Finn Graff caricature of Vladimir Putin as a
lemur touches, physically, a middling Kippenberger postcard. It's
like that up and down the walls, from top to bottom, down to the
wainscoting where the stickers begin. Yes, I said Kippenberger.
There's a Kippenberger there. There's a Valie Export photograph.
We have a garish but good little Shearer of a metalhead standing
on a ridge, gazing over the mountains.

•

It's in relation to The Hills's art collection that another of the regulars, Tom Sellers, comes into the picture. Tom Sellers is the polar opposite of the Pig. Sellers was in Düsseldorf and Cologne (right place) at the right time, and became a figure in the scene around Kippenberger, so they say. Sellers has always denied that: such Kippenberger connections are double-edged swords. Sellers has never been an artist himself; he's not interested. But like everyone who was a "figure" in "the scene around Kippenberger," he carries a hint of the aura from there, and he certainly knows several of the other "figures" from the scene—meaning he also has access to this piece or that, which most people do not. A good number of the best works donated over the past fifteen to twenty years are hanging here thanks to Tom Sellers. It was he who gave us the simple little Werner Tübke drawing of a foot hung above one end of the bar. His crowning glory is the tiny Victor Hugo watercolor of an octopus above a castle in the Rhine Valley, made using soot, coffee, and coal dust. Through his donations, Sellers has built up a considerable amount of goodwill here. His contributions, however, come with a sidecar, a protuberance, an *avec*—a pendant of slacking, disorder, and unruliness. But there's a place for that at The Hills. We should be tolerant here, says M. Hill, the General Manager. I do agree. Some days I don't.

There are also portraits of past regulars on the walls. In addition to being a personality (finance, culture, academia), you also have to spend both time and a pretty penny here. The actor (blown, bankrupt) hasn't qualified for a portrait, and considering the fines he was given after the forgery scandal, the question remains how much he'll be able to spend in the future. A portrait of the Pig also glitters in its absence, but for other reasons: the Pig offered a polite no when the General Manager suggested it may be time for a portrait. The Pig has good taste. He's certainly interested in art. Rumor has it he has a wonderful Kittelsen at home. "You know," the Pig said to M. Hill, according to the Bar Manager, "when you've studied Carl Larsson's dry points like I have all these years, well, it's a bit tricky to find a portrait artist who . . . well, you understand. You know . . . now, today. But thank you."

YOUNG LADY

THE LATECOMER STILL HASN'T ARRIVED WHEN I serve the Pig's meal.

"Would you be so kind as to check whether our friend has made an appearance in the cloakroom? A young girl . . . lady," he says quietly.

"Certainly," I say.

The Pig pulls out his phone and shows me a picture of the girl. Very unlike the Pig. What kind of tastelessness is this? There's a small queue by the cloakroom desk. They're all older, and men. Since "young" and "girl . . . lady" is the description, it doesn't look good. Old Pedersen is handling men's jacket after men's jacket.

"Is there anyone here to meet Mr. Graham?" I ask. Four don't react, and one shakes his head. I ask Pedersen, but he hasn't seen anyone. I go out onto the street and look towards the tram stop, then down in the direction of Parliament. My eyes move over the so-called dance hole, a small dip in the ground in which old

Widow Knipschild once tripped. She stumbled and had to take long steps to avoid falling, swinging her arms from side to side like some kind of razzle-dazzle, hence the name "dance hole"; all the waiting staff saw it. It's late November, and though it's a glorious day, I can't quite take it in. Habit is like a blanket which settles over the nature of things, so they say. The city is colorless despite the brilliant autumn sun, always the same, banal.

"I didn't find her."

"Hmm."

The Pig grants himself a slow sip of white burgundy. Blaise's eyes are fixed on him.

"Let me know if there's anything else," I say.

In the thirteen years I've worked here, I've never seen anyone be short-tempered or unpleasant in the Pig's company, but Blaise is speaking to the Pig with a firm tone now. And the Pig, who couldn't by any means be described as yielding or weak, is making a series of apologetic gestures. Eventually, at 2:22, Blaise stands up so abruptly that his chair toots against the floor; he throws down his linen napkin and walks towards the exit with stiff, business administration steps. I glance at the Bar Manager to make sure she has seen it—she has, like always—before I move forward and cross a line by placing my hand between the shoulder blades of a slightly flustered Pig. Katharina is still sitting, stabbing at the nuts and seeds before she mechanically puts her things back into the handbag and silently gets up.

"Is everything OK here?"

"Indeed," says the Pig.

"Would you like anything else?"

"No thank you. I'll take the bill."

The Pig plucks at his wad of cash and Vanessa clears the table, slightly too soon, slightly too hectically. None of the three have finished their meal, and the white burgundy will have to be poured away; the bottle is still half full of golden drops. I take that job: I'm happy to pour white burgundy down the drain. Grape juice from Aloxe-Corton vanishes into the sewer. The Pig remains in his seat with one soft hand on top of the other, waiting for me to return with the change that he is only going to give back to me anyway, but I let him continue his little ritual of pushing the change dish towards me and saying "You keep that," after which I will thank him deeply for the tip, the *Trinkgeld*, which was traditionally money the waiter could use to drink at the end of his shift. But I don't drink much, and my shifts go on and on. The Pig shakes down one trouser leg and goes out with his slightly warped back.

"Not every day the Pig gets stood up," says the Bar Manager.

"You can say that again," I say.

"There's a first time for everything."

"I don't like first times."

•

As though on cue, the Maître d' appears. He's always on the scene whenever there's a whiff of trouble. "What's going on?" he asks.

He'll snoop now. He has to be in control. He thinks he owns the place, possibly because his father used to be the Maître d' here, and his father before him. I tell him the truth, with a neutral face, that I'm not sure. He stares at me for a long moment and, like usual, slowly brings his big face closer to mine. As a rule, a child's face is a pure, rounded surface, the bearer of symbolic features: the eyes and the mouth. The eyes and mouth are prominent on a child's face. The eyes and mouth can be the source of fascinating beauty, an interface for communication: you can read uncertainty, joy, and sorrow in them. But with age, the face becomes more and more dominated by *the face itself*, and the eyes and mouth are thrown into the background. The Maître d's face is a striking example of this "triumph of the visage." His eyes, which I'm sure were sparkling and clear at one point in time, are not only sunken and colorless; they're also oddly small in relation to the total surface area of his face. The eye bags beneath them make as much of a statement as his eyes. Where his eyes and mouth were once responsible for the majority of expression when he was younger, they now make a minimal contribution to whatever else is "going on" on his face. His mouth, once bursting, potent, and soft, is tight and lipless, surrounded by vertical lines which make him look like he is constantly playing the flute. What is left of his "lips" now function more like shutters over his yellowed teeth. He has plenty of forehead, jaw, and cheek, with hollows, pores, and furrows, rough and slippery areas, oily surfaces. His face contains a wealth of shades and nuances, small webs of broken blood vessels, wear and tear from years of shaving, slapping on aftershave, plus alcohol consumption. Certain expressions and grimaces have taken hold. It's easy enough to see on the outside what's going on within, regardless of how "buttoned-up" he is.

"Happiness and unhappiness live side by side," he says.

Now, I can't really talk when it comes to the face. If I want to meet my own concerns head-on, so to speak, then it's just a case of looking in the mirror. It's as though my face is a cast of all the concerns that have built up within me over the years: the concerns are the mold for my face. I often feel tension and I know what it does to my face: tissue and subcutaneous fat are swept away by worries. I can feel the corners of my mouth being dragged down. A pull on my face, that's what I've got. I feel the emotions tearing at my face. How can they do it? It's understandable that a drink problem can wear out and ruin a face; it's logical that the blood vessels and pores are widened by the alcohol; you can see all that playing out in the Maître d's face drama. But the idea that emotions can ruin a face—that seems unfair. If you're nervous, you end up with a so-called nerve face. Is the face some kind of hand puppet for the nerves? It's clear that we communicate using our faces, but if we try to conceal our nerves with a poker face and still end up with a nerve face, what good comes of that? What kind of evolutionary dead end is that? You help a child when it cries, but you run when the nerve face enters. No one helps nerve face.

"Sometimes," says the Bar Manager, "the Maître d' goes around the corner there to apply face cream. Hence the sheen." I must laugh.

"He hides it well, but I can hear him rubbing it in," says the Bar Manager. We chuckle about that, the Bar Manager and me. Audibly rubbing in. "But that," says the Bar Manager, "isn't something we can let Sellers and his group, for example, get wind of. They could spin an entire architecture of mocking out of a detail like that."

•

Not long after three, a young woman comes in through the blanket curtains. She walks straight over to me and asks for Graham, aka the Pig. Her voice is at once soothing and sharp, and she manages to squeeze a series of confirmations out of me. Graham has gone? Yes. Were there others there? Yes. Was there a middle-aged man with him? There was.

The girl looks like her picture; I feel a faint sense of déjà vu. She is as thick, or should I say thin, as a lifestyle magazine. Her self-confidence and air of naturalness could easily be mistaken for intelligence, and maybe it *is* intelligence. She looks like debauchery dressed as asceticism. This may sound hair-raising, so forgive me, but I get the feeling that a person like her is a product of misogyny—and I mean that in a positive sense.

Not to be quirky here, but if you're familiar with Mathias Stoltenberg's portrait of the fifteen-year-old Elise Tvede, the one with the good mind, from Tvedestrand, it's something like that. The girl in front of me might be a lighter version of Tvede. A version with fewer tangible concerns in her life. And surrounded by a kind of deafening contemporaneity, I suppose you could say, with everything that involves. She is wearing an excellent Dries van Noten, and carries it without effort, which is afforded to very few. Her feet are strapped into flawless Aquazzura shoes, with colorful little pom-poms at the ends of the laces. But, as they say, I think that behind all the elegance, there rests an *undethronable tackiness*. I believe this girl could be described as a good, even if I'm not sure what that's supposed to mean. What kind of figure are we dealing with here? The Hills is not the place for young blood. Is she the Pig's new flagship or something?

The Pig is careful with everything bordering on the tasteless, including the opposite sex. You can observe a steady supply of well-maintained women around him, but they're always of the established variety. Not the kind who carry the harsh glow of aspiration, in other words, and not the kind who crane their necks and possess a greedy ambition in there somewhere. A woman who spends time with the Pig is a woman who has already mastered the game, a woman who does not give the impression of "needing" the Pig and whom the Pig cannot "use" at all—a woman who is the Pig's equal.

But the specimen standing in front of me here is a little young, is she not? Could she be a family member?

"Was there anything else?" I ask.

The girl stares at the mosaic on the floor. In the middle of each tile circle there are three stylized peonies in the palest of pinks. She looks up and suddenly seems ten years older.

"No, I'll come back. You can say I was here."

"Graham won't be back before tomorrow. Are you a Graham?"

"What?"

"Nothing. I beg your pardon."

The girl has a cold glow, and when she thanks me and goes, she leaves behind a so-called personality vacuum, an absence which feels palpable. The Hills dims a couple of notches when she disappears through the curtain. As my friend Edgar often says, that kind of lumbar represents the last bastion of utility value. The Maître d' comes over and takes my arm, which is relatively awkward, since I consistently hold my cards to my chest in a work context. "You shouldn't jump so high that you trip on your own beard," he says, gesturing with one hand that I have a job to do. I glance over to the Bar Manager. She has a questioning look on her face. Doesn't she know who the girl is? It's rare for the Bar Manager to be at a loss about the guests. Her mental map of Oslo's café- and restaurant-goers is exhaustive. The Bar Manager is like an encyclopedia. She takes an interest in and researches the clientele at The Hills like it is an academic field, or maybe some kind of hobby. She has catalog knowledge of the diners. She behaves like a vinyl collector when it comes to who comes and goes. Her expertise can be irritating, in the way vinyl collectors are irritating, or in the way men with a deep knowledge of, say, bikes are irritating, or men in photography shops, men "completely nerding out." To be fair, it should be said that the Bar Manager occasionally shares information that I enjoy. Never use, but enjoy in some sneaky way. But now she's standing there like the embodiment of a shrug.

EVERY MORNING

REGULARITY AND SERVICE ACT AS A BULWARK against inner noise. I work as much as I can. My days might seem endless, but that's how I want them. Every morning begins with me putting on my waiter's jacket. I take the white jacket from its hanger in the cramped changing room behind the kitchen. In with one arm, then the other. Shrug it onto my shoulders. Do up the buttons. Always the same. Sheer routine. I've had the jacket for eight years, minimum. We get our jackets from a manufacturer in Belgium which also makes military shirts. The jackets are of the highest quality, made from the same type of thin, plain-weave cotton canvas as the military shirts, and they're just as hard wearing. The jackets have a row of twenty-five-millimeter horn buttons on the front, plus two small pockets. I use the right one exclusively for the bottle opener; the left one is usually empty. The jackets do show wear, but in the nice way robust clothing does; the quality of The Hills's interior is found again in the jackets. Both The Hills and these jackets are from a time when things had to be durable and settle through use. Find their form. Not useless and disposable, like most things today. "The adornment of a city is manpower, of a body beauty, of a soul wisdom, of an object durability, of a speech truth," Gorgias writes in the *Encomium of Helen*. The part about the body is the only one which still applies, it seems. The durability of objects has been thrown overboard, at least. Some hold up; the tools the head chef surrounds himself with are durable—all of them. He avoids replacing things. As far as I know, he owns zero electronics. The fact that you constantly have to buy new electronics means that they aren't reliable. Electronics are a source of endless aggravation. We have the jackets washed and pressed three times a week, and the aesthetic span arising between a durable but worn piece of clothing and the rinsing and pressing of it, plus any possible starching, is irresistible. They use the same jackets at De Pijp in Rotterdam, Majestic in Porto, and Fuet in Badalona, as well as at the old Kronenhalle in Zürich. The waiter's jacket is standard dress, and that suits me fine.

It's not so easy, the whole clothes thing. What do I wear when I'm not at work? Normal clothes. Deeply ordinary clothes. As Edgar says: the fact you have to get dressed every day means that, every day, you have to say yes to the aesthetic choices made by a random fashion designer, high or low on the ladder, on either a good or a bad day. I often agree with Edgar, even if his reflections can be a bit grandiose. When I wear normal clothes, either on the way to or from work, I find myself falling into such a pattern of thought. My attention moves from the random designer behind the design of my underwear to the man (usually a man) who has designed my marine-blue socks, the person who came up with my tank top undershirt, the everyday shirt on top of it, my trousers. I picture the designers. There they are, on good or bad days, designing clothes which I might pull up my legs or over my head before I go out, through town, heading straight to The Hills and home again, and in a way I'm giving them publicity, these clothes and their creators. I parade their business concepts all around town. That's not something I'm comfortable with. I'm not saying I'm much to look at, and I dress as neutrally as possible, but around one conference table or another, in one office or the next, the word "neutral" has been given as the designer's motivation for this piece of clothing, and here I am, showing off this wretched designer's idea of neutrality, and that kind of thinking can make me all hectic. And as though that weren't enough, my thoughts then move on to shoes, watches, handrails, and so on, into town, until that attitude also takes over facades, display windows, road networks, food, movies, etc. And I walk around simmering away in my own mess, convinced that everyone is caught in a trap weaved from everyone else's more-or-less successful aesthetic choices and clever ideas. Business ideas, pure and simple, conceived during more-or-less successful working days, and always driven by money. And it's this money-driven lobster trap that I'm caught in. I wrap myself in a herring net of unnecessary business ideas every single day. I'm innocent in all of this. Not once have I asked for such a transaction, and not once have I forced such a transaction on anyone else. Now I sound just like Edgar.

•

As a result, when I get to The Hills at 6:45 every morning, I can free myself from my "self-chosen," "neutral" clothes. I peel them off and pull on my uniform. It gives me breathing space. My relationship with the waiter's jacket is clear, because it has a time-tested design, with deep roots in tradition, meaning that it doesn't have to express some odd, cash-whipped jacket designer's generic idea of "now," "normality," or anything like that. I like the waiter's jacket, and I left it on a hanger in the back room yesterday, as neatly as possible, so that it would be ready to wear today. Ready to be pulled on, every morning, on the dot. We go through the kitchen and into the wardrobe corner of the cramped changing room one by one and pull on our jackets. All the waiters and chefs take it in turn, aside from the Maître d'. He arrives ready dressed. I think he thinks the wardrobe corner is a bit nasty, a bit cramped, which it is.

The kitchen at The Hills resembles a forge more than a kitchen: it's burnt, carbonized. The gas flame the head chef has burning in the corner looks like a furnace. The torching and sizzling has climbed up the walls and into every nook and cranny. His helpers stand at the other end; I don't have much interaction with them. There is an opening between the kitchen and the restaurant, a mixture of a hatch and some kind of kitchen island. It isn't something that was designed: it has grown organically over the past half century, through use and additions. It's difficult to tell what's wall, what's shelf, what's pan hook, and what's bench or serving counter. The ceiling is as black as coal. The chef sweats away beneath a ceiling so opaque that you don't even see it; it's virtually gone. There are more pots and pans and other tools hanging above him, and above those is the ceiling, but you can't see that. He has stood there, the chef, flambéing and flambéing, and burnt away the ceiling, so to speak. There's an absence above the chef's spot, a void, a hollow above. That's how sooty it is. The ceiling reflects nothing. The kitchen is relatively small, and the chef stands in the spot where the head chef stood before him, and the one before him, and has always stood, frying up this and that all day long, and not least flambéing those endless flambés.

His knives are lying clean and ready on a cloth to the right of the well-used chopping board. There aren't too many of them; each one has a limited area of use. From an aesthetic point of view, they are a constant in relation to the chef's robust build, while the purity of their steel stands in sharp contrast to his harried face— something which links him, visually, even closer to the knives, possibly paradoxically, but that's how it is. He's heavy-handed and lacks the gift of the gab, as they say. He's as big as a blacksmith himself, a boor with a God-given but flat-bridged nose for gastronomy, a gorilla super-taster. He doesn't say much. When he first speaks, he's stiff and harsh. Like the time he mumbled that in the Maître d' a civil war between alcohol and homosexuality is being fought.

•

I wipe the marble surfaces. I wipe them even if they've already been wiped. I spread starched tablecloths onto the underlays and straighten them out with my hands. I bring out water. I write the day's specials in chalk on the old board by the side of the kitchen hatch. I feel like a teacher when I do that. The papers have to be brought in. It's my job to sort them out every morning and to put the long wooden clip onto the spines of each, the so-called *Zeitungsspanner.* I hang them on the newspaper rail by the entrance. We don't offer the Norwegian daily papers in a place like this; they're too primitive. We try to maintain a Continental standard. Instead, we hang the few international papers still available in printed editions. Not that we're desperately Continental, but, unfortunately, offering the Norwegian papers isn't an option. They don't abide by the duty to provide information. From time to time, when it's quiet in here, I read one of the papers by the bar. There's no plowing through it on my part. I read carefully and turn the crisp pages slowly. Slowly making your way through the crisp pages of a broadsheet is an activity which, from a purely aesthetic point of view, is related to tailoring or the saxophone. In other words, to a bygone era. Totally passé—over. Reserved for those with special interests. But it works perfectly. Call me old-fashioned, but changing what cannot be improved is also known as decline.

It's clean when I arrive at work. "Clean." The floors and surfaces are washed every night, but The Hills is in every respect a grubby restaurant. Ingrained. Not unhygienic, exactly, but it has to be said that it is a bit grimy in here, overgrown. All the years of food and fumes and breathing have essentially taken hold of the walls and formed a kind of film over the furniture and the little mosaic tiles, not to mention the ceiling. People used to smoke indoors, as one might remember, and the interior of The Hills still bears the remnants of hundreds of thousands of smoked cigarettes, from decade upon decade of smoking. The glasses and carafes are of the highest quality, traditional, not over-designed and snazzy. The cutlery, as I might have already mentioned, is early Gebrüder Hepp, or original Puiforcat. The crockery has the characteristic Hills emblem in a Delft-blue glaze, with the perfectly drawn *H* wrapped in an oval at the top. I feel vigilant every time I place these plates on a table. That's what happens with good quality. It gives you vigilance.

PART II

EDGAR AND ANNA

I'M NOT HUGELY FOND OF MIXING ROLES, BUT I have got used to the following: a good friend of mine—well, one of my main friends, Edgar, who I mentioned before; my best friend, actually—comes here roughly every second day. He always appears in the late afternoon, around 5:00 p.m., and always with his daughter, Anna. I serve them like I do everyone else, but the air between us is different. To them, I'm both their waiter and friend. We always chat, or rather they talk to me while I work. Both are fairly talkative; Edgar is good at having opinions.

Edgar and I have known one another since we were seven or eight. He's the person I've known longest. I always give Edgar and Anna the four-person table beneath the Per Krohg dog, so that Anna, who is nine, has space to do her homework to the side of the plates. A café table is, in many respects, the opposite of a school desk. Right? It's been said that the café table has been the most important place for "bohemianist research" throughout European cultural history, the very place for a self-determined, autonomous study into how and when "real life" is lived; alternatively, how life is "really lived." *Research friendships* have been struck and faded at the café table. Anna pulls out books and a pencil case, sharpens her pencil until the shavings scatter, and gets to work. Despite Edgar's caustic opinions around having children—"Norway definitely needs more allergic iPhone users"—he is fond of the girl. He has sole custody of her. The mother lives elsewhere, in another city. She's bipolar, got herself a serious benzodiazepine addiction, and had her parental rights taken away following a period of eccentric and risky behavior while Anna was a baby. I remember that Edgar was concerned about the mother's benzo intake during the first trimester of pregnancy. Some reports suggest that the use of diazepam increases the risk of cleft lips and palates. Anna has barely seen her mother. She does not, however, have a cleft palate; quite the opposite.

Anna stares at the bankrupt actor and whispers something to Edgar. The actor has a grotesque, unruly frizz transitioning into a frizz beard. He looks like a Leonberger that's been drinking spirits for one hundred years. Edgar explains that they've been watching a program in which various celebrities have to try to teach a class of seventh graders. Some of them manage it well; others make a mess of it. Anna listens intently as Edgar tells me this, and grins when he gets to the parts she finds funny. Teeth grow at different rates at that age, something which also applies to Anna. Her teeth are brilliant white, regardless of the angle or the length. I know that some children have slightly yellowed enamel on their new teeth, and that's not always quite so charming. Yellowed teeth in a messy row, in a mouth full of obnoxiousness—I can do without that. Anna is polite and well kept. Edgar is good at looking after her; I think he does the caring himself. I met Anna's friend Carl Fredrik once; he came here with them. He wasn't too polished, let me tell you. Anna laughs loudly, and her laughter is so genuine that it's hard not to let yourself be charmed. She's as sharp as a knife. There are a few golden years between infancy and the teenage period, Edgar says, when kids are as smart as they're ever going to be, or that's how it seems, when they're still uncorrupted. A huge amount of resources are put into corrupting children at that age, according to Edgar. One institution and business model after another is established solely to tame them and make their potential predictable, the limitless potential that a child still possesses when they're eight, nine, ten, or eleven years old, going to school, or sitting there being invaded by one automation or the next. School grinds them down, Edgar always says. Organized activities bend and twist the kids in certain directions; their parents force them into one mold after another. Technology makes its presence known and does its best to "take" children from an early age; it presents itself as the law of nature and pulls and tears at children with its temptations and illusions, trickling into their nervous systems, into their DNA, so that it, the technology, really does become the law of nature, meaning the children can rarely or never again stand or sit with their full, uncorrupted potential, laughing loudly, straight from their bellies, the way Anna does now, as Edgar talks about the TV program.

Anna is *on her feet*—he's that funny. She points at him and laughs because one of these celebrity-cum-teachers, Edgar says, had the misfortune of letting out the pupils' speckled dwarf hamster, which led to complete chaos. The children squeal and run euphorically around the classroom, climbing the walls and falling over. The TV crew must have filmed it at high speed, because there are scenes cut in here and there, in extreme slow motion, crystal clear images of chairs tipping over and pencil sharpeners opening in midair, with their contents—the shavings—going everywhere. A desk tips over, and you can actually see a handful of crumbs from erasers— rubbings—*scatter* across the floor at macro level. Anna is completely absorbed. The celebrity teacher shuffles around, stooped, trying to get hold of the little animal, which is running in terror from corner to corner. She is crosscut with seven other celebrities all struggling to keep their respective classes in line. Edgar says that he doesn't know who any of these people are, apart from two of them: one is an old folk singer he remembers from his childhood, and the other is the poor, broke actor eating three tables away. The program must have been filmed before his forgery was uncovered: he looks fresher and more in shape on the TV screen than in real life, Edgar says. I've always thought that The Hills is a good place for Anna to sit, away from the organizing, the screens, the monitoring, the schooling, and the taming. The Maître d' is a hawk, though: he comes over, apropos pencil shavings, and says that I need to sweep up the shavings which have fallen beneath Anna—or "the girl," as he calls her.

COFFEE

COFFEE AND MOTORING HAVE, IN A SLIGHTLY
unobvious sense, reached the same proportions and the same
metaphysical union with a "free Western life," I've occasionally
thought when I'm in a philosophical mood, possibly influenced by
Edgar. The morning, as we all know, belongs to coffee. Regardless of the ripple effects that coffee production and motoring have,
it's hard to imagine a life without the two, ideally in combination,
and preferably in the morning. The activities of slurping coffee and
driving cars are, in one's very chromosomes, linked to the idea of
getting pumped up and under way. The image of the bittersweet
early morning with a coffee, or in the car, or with a coffee in the
car, or with the car parked up outside the coffee place to get a
coffee to have in the car, or the old European café coffee, which
isn't linked to the car as such but should be viewed as some kind of
transportation stage, which is also a destination in itself, the same
way the car is always a transportation stage and an end station in

itself. Doing away with one of these is like amputating a limb from the body of society: it's completely out of the question. It's hard to see how the machinery of society is meant to "get going" every morning without the two. "Decaffeinated coffee is like kissing your sister," someone once said. Isn't it typical that the only coffee quote I know is about decaffeinated coffee? The Bar Manager has put her foot down when it comes to serving decaf. It's not possible, she says. She's not some coffee fanatic, no coffee Nazi—she doesn't have any warped barista ideology—but she is part of the old school, and the line has to be drawn somewhere, she claims.

Morning is mainly about coffee here at The Hills. It can also be about croissants with jam and the morning papers, but the coffee itself is the crux of the morning's activities. The Bar Manager is of the opinion that the cultural significance of coffee, not snobbish but its actual value, in terms of both history and *Realpolitik*, should shine through our serving rituals. I myself have to be very careful with my coffee intake, but it's difficult to break the habit of a cup in the morning, especially since you end up distancing yourself from an important community if you don't spend your early mornings sipping coffee. Decaffeinated coffee is a surrogate for the feeling of belonging, pure and simple. You can still nurture the image of yourself as a coffee-sipping individual if the coffee is decaffeinated, but coffee is very much about caffeine, let's just put that out there; it's not just aesthetics and scene. Just think of *Schweigt stille, plaudert nicht*—Johann Sebastian

Bach's Coffee Cantata, which Johansen regularly plays up there on the mezzanine. I've heard that Voltaire drank fifty cups of coffee a day. I get very shaky from coffee. Sometimes it tips over to sheer paranoia. My so-called high sensitivity isn't a good fit with caffeine; it's one of the stimulants we highly sensitives react most strongly to. Other things we highly sensitives react to are noise and complex social contexts. The mixing of roles. And hunger, or being given too many jobs to do at once. We can also quickly become *drained* in interactions with others, rather than gaining energy from them. I can't drink coffee before I get to work in the morning. The sounds, the chatter of the guests—it all becomes too sharp. I quickly start to feel dizzy and get palpitations if I drink too much coffee; I get the feeling of internal collapse.

This isn't the place to bring up personal history, but I remember one morning a few years back, a morning like today, the same time of year, with the same sunlight as now, falling obliquely into the restaurant over the coffee cups and morning papers on the worn marble tabletops. I'd felt uppish and had been stupid enough to drink three or four cups of coffee before twelve. I swung behind the bar, loaded the machine, and made myself one espresso after another. The intake of more caffeine can curb the comedown after too much coffee, and I had kept up that curbing all morning, with the help of repeated espresso consumption. When it was approaching half past one I went to top up the cup of a gentleman sitting beneath the longest mirror, on the east wall. My job has two key criteria: I have to show *pride in my work*, and I have to be *self-effacing*. The pride in my work makes me adhere to rigid routines which are vital for my well-being, since being highly sensitive means that I don't like surprises or change. The self-effacing aspect means that I can interact with and serve people without having to get involved. In times like these, when the majority of poses are tasteless, it seems that responsibility, pride in work, and being self-effacing are things one should nurture. So, with the coffeepot in hand, proud and self-effacing, I go over to the man sitting beneath the mirror on the long wall. He's wearing the tie from hell, I'd almost say. The pattern on it is so busy that I lose my momentum and simply stand in front of him for a few seconds, completely unable to mobilize any of my standard phrases. And, slightly puzzled by my silence as he stiffly asks for a refill, I experience a collapse, primarily caused by his tie. I still think that: that it was his tie which caused it. The tie was an improbable weave of three shades of blue: an almost grayish Cambridge blue as the base, interspersed with stripes of Tufts blue and topped with speckles of what might have been periwinkle. The sight of his tie slams into my retinas and makes, physically, this house of cards of a nervous system that I was dealt, and which has been fundamentally destabilized by my coffee drinking, come crashing down, and I fall inwards, a slide and a fall; I collapse internally. Everything becomes bright, and my head grows and becomes light as a helium balloon; it feels like my head is rising, but it's falling, "it" is falling, everything inside me is falling, and I have to grip the side with my free hand to avoid tipping over. My hand brushes against an old woman's cheek and bumps her table, making the cups rattle and the tea slosh as she sits cackling with her friend, completely unaware that I, her waiter, would come staggering in from one side like a character from a silent film and practically slap her soft, wrinkled cheek. I regain my balance, but don't dare apologize, since my mouth feels completely lopsided and my tongue thick and back-heavy. If I try to speak now, I'll make it worse by following the cheek slapping and tea spilling with the sounds of a dog or a bear. So I stand there, blinking, still with the coffeepot in my hand, and now I feel some kind of adrenaline rush rising inside; it gives me a slight lift. The man with the tie looks like he's swallowing a series of bitter belches.

"Refill?" I say, amazed that words and not howls are coming out. My upper arms are tingling, and I quickly glance at the hand holding the coffeepot.

"No thank you," says the man. It's there, my hand: I can see it but can't feel it; it's numb, completely gone.

"I'll get someone to clean up," I say to the old woman, before walking out into the kitchen with broad, acute psychiatric steps, as though to find my sea legs against the dizziness. The little Filipino man with the floppy ears who did the washing up back then runs away with a cloth as I say the words "spill" and "table fourteen." What was his name again? I stand on the inside of the swinging door, breathing through my nose and squeezing my hands until I regain the feeling in them. Bayani, I think it was, Baiany, Bajanwi. The chef is flambéing repetitively beneath the carbonized ceiling.

He pours cognac into the sauté pan and deftly catches a flame from the gas hob so that a fireball is thrown up from the copper pan. The blue alcohol flame against the golden copper looks amazing. He's an aesthete, the chef. These days, I try to limit my coffee consumption to the afternoon, or the evening.

EYEBALLS

WHAT DO YOU KNOW: HERE SHE COMES, IN THE same morning light, across the mosaic tiles, in relaxed, low shoes. The young woman the Pig and his company were waiting for the other day. This early? Is it breakfast she wants? Now, I may be in disarray, but it feels like some kind of "bidding round" takes place every time she comes in. Isn't it called a Giffen good, a product which paradoxically becomes more in demand as its price rises? It's like the young woman has a similar quality. I don't know.

She sits down and glances over to me as I stand here, blossoming in my waiter's uniform. Or "blossoming" isn't the word: I'm standing still; I stand here year after year, getting older, more like moss. She moves her head back almost imperceptibly. What do you call a nod that goes backwards? Raising the chin. She raises her chin to me, and what a chin. I react quickly and go over with two menus beneath my arm.

"Are you expecting company?"

"No."

"Coffee?"

"Yes, please."

For a moment I think about asking whether she got hold of the Pig, Graham, but I bat that away, slightly shocked that I'm even considering it. It's way beyond my job description to press and question the guests. Suddenly you end up putting your foot in it. She could be a grandchild; she could be a business contact or an erotic liaison, for all I know. The guests shouldn't have to explain themselves in here. But you do think about things. She must be some kind of asset, otherwise she wouldn't be in circulation. A resource for the Pig. Credit. What does the Bar Manager know about her? Very little, it seems. She stands there with her intelligent face looking like a question mark.

It seems unfair that we always have to describe appearance first when describing girls, but what can I do? It's all I have. When you look up at a clear sky, focus plays no part. What would you focus on? It's the same with this girl, I think: you can clearly see her, she's clear, but she's never in focus. I don't really know. The impression she gives is absorbing. I hand her one of the menus, clutching the other to my ribs. I stand there for a bit too long; she's reading, and I'm staring straight at the top of her head—her crown, I suppose it's called. A not-quite-straight part in her hair runs from this crown down to her left temple, where her fringe is pushed to the right and then falls over her face. She is leaning forward, studying the menu.

Edgar had an affair with a girl once. She drove him crazy.
Even though she always showed complete affection, Edgar said,
and showered him with the sense that he was supreme in a way he
had never experienced with any other partner—he had believed
her and her shower of compliments completely—he was also eaten
up by the suspicion that he wasn't the only one being given that
treatment.

"Could I have a little milk in my coffee?" the girl says with
some kind of smile.

Edgar never managed to prove anything. He never caught her
flirting or cheating in any way, but the fact that her radiance had
had such a magical effect on him from the very outset could only
mean, Edgar argued, that it also had a similar effect on others. And
the thought that she, that person, that *being*, who had made him
feel so unique, perhaps for the very first time, might not actually
have been exclusively his, made him boil over. The fact that she
struck *him* in that special way, and might potentially strike all the
others in the same way, made him short-circuit. The greediest,
most egotistical, and unkind sides of Edgar came out then, he has
said, and grew uncontrollably, like weeds, like wheatgrass, with
their long, creeping, and far-reaching roots. He related to her the
way a capitalist relates to his money pot, he said. Like a hawker.
Stingy. I never met her, but I've developed an image of her in my
mind—from the hours I spent listening to Edgar's woes at the
time—and that image materializes in the young woman sitting
before me here at The Hills. She's just how I imagined her. A

generator for jealousy. The girl looks up at me, and I realize that she's wondering what happened to the coffee, because now she hands me the menu and asks for the cereal with linden honey and goat yogurt.

"And the coffee, too."

I hurry out to the kitchen, my back straight. It might sound funny, but that's exactly what I do: I hurry across the floor. I hurry through the swinging doors and out into the kitchen, grab one of the coffeepots, and immediately return with it in one hand and a petite steel milk jug in the other. The jug is so small that I have to hold the handle between my thumb and index finger. I rush over to the young lady and pour the coffee. Then I subtly lift the milk jug while I look at her and raise my eyebrow almost imperceptibly, as though to suggest the question *Would you like a drop of milk in your coffee?*

"Yes, please," she replies to that gestural question, and I pour an amount of milk which couldn't be described as anything but a dash. I give her another questioning look and she says, "A little more," and I, standing with my back angled, with my little finger pointing upwards and out because of the tiny jug, pour another dash.

"One moment, and I'll fetch you the day's paper," I say, but she stops me and says that it's not necessary.

"Wonderful," I say.

Really? Not interested in the papers in the morning? I see. I can sometimes be blinded by the notion of old Europe that's being nurtured and conserved here at The Hills, but I'm still taken aback that she can't yield to the tradition of rustling a broadsheet over a coffee in the morning light. What does she mean it's not necessary? Physical newspapers are increasingly swapped for other equipment in here, even in the morning, I've noted that. I'm not saying there's any kind of betrayal in fishing out a device rather than rustling the paper; all I'm saying is that it's noted. But the young lady doesn't pull out one form of technology or another. She just sits there as though on exhibit, sipping her coffee with calm movements.

•

As I walk around scraping crumbs, I follow the girl out of the corner of my eye, taking in everything she does or, more accurately, everything she doesn't do. She continues her sipping, but otherwise there's very little to write home about. My favorite activity is actually using the crumber to scrape the crumbs from the tables. We have both crumbers and so-called crumb brushes at the restaurant; I prefer the crumber. I deftly push the crumbs onto the crumb tray I'm holding beneath the edge of the table. I hang the crumber back in its place and go over to the young woman. With the venerable *New York Times* in my hands—not some paper from the nervous, old Europe, I'll have you know, but one of the papers which, ironically enough, maintains a sense of the old Europe, the Old World, or something like that. It offers an air of the twentieth century. I hand her a fresh, crisp copy.

"That's not necessary," she says.

"Thank you," I say.

Why am I pushing newspapers onto the guests? Thank you? I put down the eternal *New York Times*, grab the crumber again, and run it over the tablecloths with experienced hands. I even run it over the tops of the tables I've already scraped, doubling the amount of work for myself.

"Excuse me," the girl says, signaling that she wants to pay. I immediately present her with the bill. While she fishes out the cash from a becomingly cluttered handbag, I suggest that it looks like a lovely day today.

"Uh," says the girl.

When she gets up, it sinks in how hideously well proportioned she is. Symmetrical. I've seen it—I saw it yesterday—but I didn't take it in. Now I take it in. There's a male guest in the middle of his forties two tables away, and he can't control his eyeballs as she straightens up and stretches—yes, she stretches—before she swings an autumn coat over her shoulders, a light jacket, a crochet jacket? A knitted jacket? Was it knitted on thick needles? Is it homemade? Was it made on a machine? An organic, long-waisted, hand-knitted sweater camouflaged as a jacket? A cozy angora? The eyeballs of the man two tables away have taken on a life of their own, that much is clear. It's interesting to watch a man whose eyeballs are out of control. How strong can eyeballs be? On the other hand, I should look at my own eyeballs before I start talking about other people's. My eyeballs are running amok just as badly as his. The difference is that my eyes are seeking out his for brief moments, as though they want to confirm that he (his eyeballs) are seeing what I (my eyeballs) are seeing. The man's eyeballs are in a fight with his will, which is trying to keep them to himself, but the eyeballs are drawn to the girl like two owlets as she stands there stretching and pulling on that slightly long crocheted jacket, whatever a jacket is called when it's slightly long. Then she walks towards the door. Her journey towards the exit sucks the air from the room, reestablishing some of that personality vacuum. With elegant, possibly self-objectivizing steps, she disappears through the curtains. She reappears on the outside of the arched windows, which are covered at the bottom with lace curtains on brass poles. She disappears behind the wall again, reappears in the next window, disappears behind the wall, and continues like that along the entire row of windows, off and on, like a film strip.

"Like all slaves, girls think they're watched more than they really are," the man with the eyeballs mutters, glancing at me. What does he mean by that? He should pull in his eyeballs so they don't roll out of his skull. I see that the swindler actor has taken his seat. And, on cue, Old Johansen starts playing the piano up on the mezzanine: he gives us Bach, and Goldberg Variation No. 5, up-tempo. These small occurrences mean that the time is almost exactly ten in the morning.

"I'll have a vodka," says the actor.

"Would you prefer Belvedere," I ask, "or Reyka?" That's the Icelandic vodka I know he drinks from time to time.

The actor breathes like a whale; it seems as though life itself leaves his body. He then sucks in air so that his nose whistles before he lets the air go again, and growls, "Belvedere," with a voice so sonorous that you might think it had seeped out from the bowels of hell.

I exchange a few words with the Bar Manager; she's the one I talk to if I have to chat. She tells me she had some unfortunate trouble with the timing belt, as it's known, in her car, right in the middle of the afternoon yesterday, plus that the Rwandan Twa people are, interestingly enough, potters, something which is unusual among Pygmy peoples; they generally trade agricultural products, iron, and pottery for meat. And—would you believe it?—the Bar Manager has managed to get her hands on a lovely little Twa pot. "Listen, the young lady—who is she?" I ask out of the blue. "The rapist," the Bar Manager says cryptically, the way she often does when she owes me an answer, "is not brawling with either man or woman, but with sexuality itself." What? She smiles and tells me that the Twa pot sits on the sideboard at home, and is of fantastic quality.

THE PIG WANTS
TO TALK

THE PIG ARRIVES AT 1:30 ON THE DOT AND SITS WITH his hands in his lap. He is too decent, too tasteful, too refined, to fiddle with his phone at all times. There's something unseasoned about checking text messages and social media. If you have to pull out your phone and check it constantly, you're a child or some kind of tart—yes, let that sound as petty as you like. Independent, balanced people with a certain status don't do that. But then I have the misfortune of telling the Pig that the young woman he was waiting for yesterday was here not just yesterday but earlier today, too, thereby forcing the venerable Pig onto his phone.

"She was here earlier today?" His eyes widen.

"Yes."

"Did she ask after me?"

"Not today."

"And yesterday?"

"Yes, she asked yesterday."

"Would you excuse me a moment?"

From the inner pocket of his suit jacket—impeccable, not the pocket of his trousers, spotless—he pulls out his phone, depraved. He starts jabbing at it. Will he call, I wonder, or will he send a message? So far so interesting. I pay attention. Is he going to make a call, or is he going to text? Will he use his fingers or his voice to communicate what needs to be communicated? He taps the glass with his fingertips. From where I'm standing, it's impossible to tell whether he's bringing up a number or whether he's typing. He half turns to me and gives a gesture which is supposed to mean *Two minutes*, before he goes off towards the exit. As he disappears behind the curtain, the heat blanket, the fabric covering the door, he lifts the phone to his ear. Interesting. I watch him outside; he even lights a cigarette. He walks up and down the street for three minutes as he breathes in tobacco smoke, drag after drag, and talks on the out breaths. His right hand, which is holding the filterless cigarette, gestures calmly between inhalations. When he comes back in, he says: "Right."

I fetch the bottle of white burgundy, which I swiftly open with the opener I keep in the right-hand pocket of my jacket, then I pour.

"There will be three of us today, not four," says the Pig. And then:

"You know, there's a thing I'd like to discuss with you."

I clear the unneeded fourth setting from the table.

"What is it?"

"I've wanted to mention it to you for a while."

"I beg your pardon?" I say as my face warms up.

"You know," says the Pig. "You know, when Peter Norton bought the letters Joyce Maynard put up for auction at Sotheby's in 1999 . . ."

"Peter Norton," I say.

"Yes, fourteen letters and notes from 1972 and 1973, in which Salinger, among other things—ironically—warns young Joyce Maynard against fame and exploitation . . ."

"I'm sorry," I say.

"Norton's intention in buying the letters—they went for well over $150,000, double the estimate—was to give them back to Salinger, so that he could do what he liked with them: lock them away in a safe, burn them . . ."

"I'm sorry," I say. "I have to see to the other tables."

"But there's something I really want to discuss with you . . ."

"Excuse me," I say.

"Norton was also after one of Holbein's more obscure Tudor drawings which was on sale at the same auction . . ."

"You'll have to excuse me."

"When does your shift finish?" asks the Pig.

"At five, but then I have to go straight to a meeting."

"I see."

I never have meetings. I'm always at work. What was that? I have to do my job now. Where's the crumber? Tables five and twelve have gone, I need to de-crumb them. I quickly clear the tables, find the crumber, and run over the tablecloths with energetic movements. Now seven and three have left. I take payment for nineteen. Table eleven wants more mineral water, and four sends back a Loosen Bros. Riesling. What was this talk about Salinger and Maynard? Holbein? The Bar Manager hints that table three will be getting new guests. The two people keeping the Pig company at his usual table ten also arrive. I escort them over; one is a colleague of the Pig's, a sharp-nosed, vulture-like figure called Årvoll; the other is his polite but slightly startled daughter. I recognize both of them from previous occasions. I fill their glasses. For thirteen years, we've kept things professional, the Pig and I. Why this sudden eagerness? A "thing"? I keep in continual motion until the clock strikes five, at which point I quickly get changed. I have to get out, away from the eager Pig, who is still sitting here, three and a half hours later—likely full of questions about Maynard and Salinger—sipping his never-ending burgundy. He studies the greasy belts of alcohol sliding down the glass. Doesn't he have anything better to do? I have to get away from the Pig's sippings.

ABUSE OF ANIMALS

"SHOULD I ASK THE CHEF TO FRY SOME ONION?" I
ask two days later.

"No thank you," says Anna.

"If you have," says Edgar. He looks at Anna and points to the
beef patties with a surprised expression.

"Beef patties," says Anna.

"Beef patties." Edgar nods.

The chef rinses the chopping board and peels, cuts, and fries
the onion. That this vegetable has been used for thousands of years
is strange, and that the ancient Egyptians *worshipped* it is hard to
believe, in my opinion. Is it because concentric skins and multiple
layers symbolize eternal life or the solar system? Onions weren't
used in cooking in the countryside where I grew up. The chef
shovels the fried onions onto a medium-sized plate, and I place it
in front of Edgar so that the restaurant logo is at precisely twelve
o'clock, if you imagine the plate as a clockface.

"Thanks," he says. "You don't want any?" I shake my head. He knows I never eat at work.

"I'm not too keen on onions."

"Me neither," says Anna.

"In the past, people thought onions made them strong," I say.

"How strong?"

"Strong. Gladiators rubbed onion onto their muscles to get stronger. In the Middle Ages, people paid their rent with onions."

"Now you're being silly," says Edgar.

"No."

"Could you pay with onions in the shop?" Anna wonders.

"I don't know. Maybe they didn't have shops. But you could get your hair back if you went bald. They made you strong. And potent."

"What's potent?" asks Anna.

"Getting erect," says Edgar.

"And think of the poor Indians. We took the onion to America," I say.

"'We'?"

"Europeans. We found potatoes, turkey, gold, and tobacco over there. And coffee. And cocaine. And bananas. We brought it all back home. And we took the onion over with us. What did the Indians make of that?"

"They probably don't like onion."

"But now there aren't any Indians," says Edgar.

"Yes, there are," says Anna. "Catarina in my class is an Indian."

"Where is she from?"

"Venezuela."

"She's probably mixed," says Edgar.

"I don't know, but she's got a lisp," says Anna.

"Thee lithpth?"

"Yeth, thee lithpth."

"The Thpanith do that, too. It meanth that thee hath Thpanith blood in her veinth. Thee'th half-blood."

"I thee," Anna says seriously.

"Venethuela," says Edgar.

Edgar rubs the bridge of his nose, making a slight smacking sound with his right eye. After that, he clears his throat and blinks until his eye focuses. Edgar is tired of me. I ask whether Anna still eats meat. Edgar points to the beef patties. Once, she talked about how meat was disgusting because of animal abuse, I say. Unappetizing, or "appa," as they said in the village. Edgar has money in the bank, I know that. He doesn't have an appendix, I know that, too. Edgar can come out with things like: *In everyday speech, meat is the muscle and fat tissue from slaughtered animals, which is sold as food for humans*, and then pull a meaningful expression, as though he's revealed something. As though he had single-handedly uncovered the perverseness of fetishizing food intake. Edgar can be so conceited. He talks away. The abuse of animals is one thing, he says. But what does that abuse say about the people looking after the animals?

It's time for an explanation. He wets his lips. Edgar takes it upon himself to talk about an article he read, about a new book written by an author whose starting point was a news report recounting the Norwegian Society for the Protection of Animals' welfare investigations into the abuse of animals on Norwegian farms. And imagine, says Edgar, the Society claims that serious abuse often testifies to the farmer's depression or mental breakdown. In other words, the neglect of animals is almost always a sign of human breakdown. The book he is referring to is a novel, and the trick in the novel—listen, says Edgar—is to depict a farmer's mental collapse *from the animals' point of view*. An *Animal Farm* of psychiatry, if you like. The farmer was a bachelor, aged forty-seven. The pigs were thirsty. Things dragged on. What was he doing? The only one who had contact with him was the cat, who moved freely in and out through the cat flap and sat on his lap. The TV was on as usual. The dog complained from its kennel. Its lead reached almost to the kitchen window, but it couldn't see in.

The sheep were freezing. It was early November. For seven whole days they had stood outside. The snow hadn't arrived yet, but there was frost in the mornings and it was bitingly cold. A couple of them had diarrhea and got muck on their wool. A border around the fence was stripped bare: the sheep had forced their heads through and ripped up all the edible stubs and roots. There were howls from the pigpen. The sow had licked and nibbled at one of the piglets so much that it was dark and looked like a seal cub. What about the hens? Two had been pecked to death, and one was featherless and covered in open sores. The other hens skipped past and dealt out heartless bites and nips. The author had done thorough research, because there were details in the book that she couldn't possibly have made up, Edgar argues. Edgar himself has worked on a farm, he says, and knows how long it takes before, for example, a horse becomes dehydrated or, say, the pigs turn on one another. The book was well written, in Edgar's opinion. Conceptually comprehensive and not at all over-the-top. And that wasn't an easy task, given that the book's point of view is the animals' and, as we know, animals have no language. How do you describe the feeling of starvation felt by a cow? Cows have five stomachs but no vocabulary. What should an author write when, through the mistreated pig's emotional register, she needs to describe confusion and fear? Edgar hadn't thought anyone would manage it before he began reading, but the author had certainly found a clever solution to that particular narrative problem. Any solution to Edgar's endless harangues is not mentioned.

TRANSPORT

I THINK WITH HORROR ABOUT ALL THE TRANSPORT, all the transportation, the truly endless transportations, which must have happened for Blaise to be sitting here, glittering— as he sits at the Pig's usual table ten—repetitively raising the espresso cup to his lips. Where does the marble beneath the tablecloth come from? Bolzano? Where is the porcelain from? Hungary? His suit is from London—or rather the stitching and cutting was done in London—but where is the *material* from? The material comes from here, the lining from there. The tie might be Scottish; it's a tartan pattern. I recognize the cuff links: they're from a big French fashion house. His shoes are from Lombardo, I've noticed, and his socks, believe it or not, I recognize as American. He has bought the socks from Neiman Marcus. And so on. I know that he, Blaise, gets his hair cut by Joao Fuentes, the Portuguese hairdresser and stylist, at a salon called Federer. The hairdresser has flown in from

Portugal, while his socks came flying from the USA. And so on. Then there's the coffee: the beans are dragged, heaved, driven, and shipped all the way from Bolivia; and it's a claustrophobic thought, that the only thing in my field of vision right now, here at The Hills, as I stand looking at Blaise and his constituent parts—the only thing from Norway is the splash of milk in the little steel jug. But the cow was still milked up in the valleys somewhere, by a farmer, mentally ill or not, and the milk, it was tanked and sloshed and jostled down the milk route towards the capital just so it could end up in the petite Gebrüder Hepp milk jug that I've placed in front of him. Everything is dragged in. The building has been here a long time, but nothing comes from this place. The overall experience of a Grand European in central Oslo is a patchwork without parallel. It's made possible by plundering items from every corner of the world; they've trawled the ends of the earth for matter and means, materials—and ideas. Because the idea itself is, of course, from Vienna, or Paris, or possibly Berlin, with one approach or another from the pubs and dives in Amsterdam or Rotterdam, to which the Norwegians have had access over the years as a result of sea travel. But at the same time, The Hills is one of the capital's defining institutions, one which gives Oslo character and draws the long lines. The space, or the premises, where I now and will forever stand in my waiter's jacket, is an intricate meshwork of scraped-together items, and I sometimes feel sick at the thought that the longest-standing, most constant and unchanging "traditional place" is a mosaic of items dragged and scraped together. This place is a conglomerate and a concentration of snatched-together items, and I often think about all the transport lines which are established, maintained, and worn out; which point to The Hills from all directions so that the plunderings can find their way here, to The Hills, and down into the cellar and up into the kitchen, to be carried by me to the tables, right over to Blaise's marble top. They point from every corner of the world, to Europe, to northern Europe, to Oslo, to The Hills. Early morning here, with this level of tradition and quality, would not be possible without the tankers, suburban depots, railway shunts, loading ramps, loading slings, trucks, bleach buckets, dinners, the transporters, pallets, and cranes. How much land and stretches of Europe and the rest of the world are torn apart, slumified, and buried under traffic, with all the wear and tear that transport brings, so that Blaise can repeatedly lift his espresso cup to his lips and feel a sense of belonging to something European, is anybody's guess. Transportation is important because it enables trade between people—so I've heard, probably from Edgar—which again leads to civilization. It's through transport that civilization is established, and it's through transport that civilization will go under, I should think, or at least that's what Edgar thinks. Anyway, I digress. Out of the cars and down into the cellar go the goods. Everything goes down to the cellar. Via the trapdoor or the loading window. The men who do the lifting push two loading rails into the hatch and let the boxes slide down. What is the name of that piece of equipment? I once asked them while they were lifting.

"What do you call those rails?"

"No idea," he said.

So the equipment has no name. Down into the cellar it goes, in any case. We have an intricate goods cellar beneath the restaurant.

SERVING ERROR

FRIGIDITY, SOMEONE ONCE SAID, IS THE TRUTH behind nymphomania. Impotence is the truth behind Don Juanism. And anorexia, well, that's the truth behind bulimia. I can't remember who said it, but I think about those words as the unstoppable, I'm close to saying, young lady who asked after the Pig makes yet another entrance. The curtain moves to one side. Here she is. "Herself," 100 percent, but also painfully generic. She's suddenly, it might seem, after only a few days, the most frequent guest at the establishment. What does she want? With a choppy, zeitgeist stride, she heads in the direction of the Maître d', who is bent over the register, fuming. She smiles with her full dental arch.

She's too early this time: it's one fifteen, a quarter before the Pig's table is set. And yet again she brings with her a feeling of déjà vu, stronger today. Her power. Her posture, the squeezing together of her shoulder blades. Her shoes. The intelligent contradiction of her outfit. She makes the room light up. My workplace immediately becomes a scene, an arena. At the same time, it's as though she drags all of The Hills' grandeur, age, and long-standing diligence down to the level of her hip bone. The Hills is an eatery, but in many ways this girl expresses a hatred of flesh, a fantasy of the fundamentals of the physique—the skeleton. She's on the phone.

"Oh God, you're *gross!*" She continues to smile.

With her hand over the receiver, she asks the Maître d' about Graham. The Maître d' tells her—with help from a mouth which is more a taut ring, a sphincter, than two separate lips, and a couple of bent fingers suggesting direction—that the Pig's table will be ready in five minutes. Could she take a seat at the bar until then?

The talkative Bar Manager, owner of a brand-new timing belt and an elegant Twa pot, is standing with her spine as straight as a spear, with her smart expression, and firmly asks what she would like. The girl gives her a blank look, as though there were water in front of her eyeballs, and places an order. And this is when the plot thickens. I pay close attention: she asks for a quadruple espresso. The Bar Manager doesn't exactly widen her eyes—she's a professional—but you can see that she has thoughts on the matter, as they say. She goes straight over to the machine and pours one espresso on top of another until it's a quadruple. I've paused with the crumber. The Bar Manager is filling an ordinary coffee cup to the brim with espresso: it's a shocking sight. The very thought of the espresso being quadruple makes me sweat. I stare at the girl's face. She sips. How to describe that sipping? In a time like ours, as Edgar says, where the existing political language is unable to offer any other solution other than keeping people's suffering at a distance through control, market expansion, concern for white people's health, extreme tourism, and entertainment, how should I describe this girl's drinking of a quadruple espresso? There is no political language to express the conflicts of our age. But this much I can say: the girl drinks the coffee as though it's *me* who should be drinking it. Does that make sense? The cup, made from quality stoneware, placed on an adorable saucer, is raised to her mouth with hypnotizing calm. The small clouds of steam or whatever it is that rises from hot coffee—it must be water vapor? Mixed with some scent particles? What is it that smells like coffee in and around the rising steam? Coffee atoms? I'm rambling. What I'm trying to say is that the vapor from the cup produces some kind of receptive, inviting "breath," which—how should I put it?—"sells" the coffee to me. The quadruple espresso is sold to me, the highly sensitive, by the espresso itself, aided by the girl's interaction with it. What kind of agent is she? What is her product? It seems like the Bar Manager needs a shot herself: she's watching just as intently as I am.

•

He's well-off, the Pig, with plenty on his plate. Some kind of prosperity in practice—that's what he does, on a day-to-day basis.

Everyone he surrounds himself with plays one role or another in this activity. It's crucial that the demonstration of this practice and maintenance of wealth is done with class. The conversation taking place between three ordinary moneymen on table seven, for example, would never be heard from the Pig's table:

"He's a fool . . . he benched the boat at thirteen. You know how much salt's on the liter? He came down with pure slush, PURE slush."

With perfect timing and a whiplash-like motion, the young girl downs the last of her coffee as the Pig comes through the curtain, with Blaise Engelbert hot on his heels. It looks like Blaise is uncomfortable with the order, as though he's never walked behind another person before. But the Pig, without being some kind of shameless alpha, has a natural authority—or is it slyness?—which means he consistently pulls his right shoulder in front of Blaise as they approach the Maître d', as they are shown to the table, as they take their seats.

I act like an idiot by saying "Voilà" to the young woman, to indicate that her company has arrived, but she's already worked that out. I, the Bar Manager, and the Maître d' stand idly by, watching her slide off the barstool, grab her "creation" of a bag, and her seamless (not literally: it does have seams) jacket. With confident, stony steps, she walks over to the Pig and his group. The Pig and Blaise spot her at the same moment; they let go of the backs of chairs and napkins and turn to her "like flowers towards the sun," as my grandmother would have put it. They are ready and waiting, and the girl hugs them in age order, meaning the Pig first, then Blaise. She isn't related to either of them, that much is clear. The fawning and fuss which the Pig and Blaise show her isn't something you do with your nearest and dearest. And a grandchild would never be so coquettish with their grandfather.

She seems rushed, breathless, as though the clock is ticking. Why such a hurry? Maybe she's buzzing from the quadruple espresso. She is like a flapping fish, fresh food demanding to be consumed, because she is approaching her expiry date with every passing moment.

The Pig's table is mine. Maybe it would have been appropriate to pull out a chair for the young lady, but I hang the crumber on its hook and start to shuffle the menus instead. "Lady," I say. It's hard to say whether she's a lady or a girl. Child or lady. She's some kind of child lady. In every respect, she's an adult. Definitely adult in appearance as well as in her habits, which are far too refined to belong to a child, not to mention expensive. And the youthful tenderness, the slightly undeveloped impression of being fresh, seems cultivated, and in a refined rather than innocent way. A professional way. Dare I say a speculative way?

"The thinnest string makes the finest music," the Maître d' says, sending me an impenetrable look from behind his eye bags. I know I have to take the drink order. The Maître d' shouldn't have to make an effort with glances and so on. I hasten over.

"What do you know," the Pig says with a smile, indicating that a bottle of white burgundy would be appropriate.

I hand out the menus clockwise. Not to boast, but the way I

elegantly open the cover with one hand, straight to the lunch page, and hand it to the Child Lady at a comfortable reading angle is both quick and smooth, experienced. She looks up at me and nods. Blaise gets his menu last. I don't open his; since he's sitting at an awkward angle to the right, Blaise gets a closed menu.

"Would you like me to go through the specials?" I say.

"No thank you," says the Pig.

"Let me just say that the plaice is very good today."

"Thank you."

Let me just say? What is it with my brazenness? Didn't the Pig say no? The plaice is completely ordinary today. What am I talking about? I go over to the bar and ask the Bar Manager for two brandies. She quickly pours two Stravecchios and I place one in front of the Pig and one in front of Blaise. The Pig politely turns to me as he takes off his menu glasses.

"What is this?" he says.

"Stravecchio," I say.

"What?"

I feel a tic in my neck and apologize, say, "I'm so sorry, it must be a mistake." A serving error. I shake my head, pick up the glasses of brandy, and return them to the bar.

"Was it off?" the Bar Manager asks. She opens the Stravecchio and sniffs it. With my jaws grinding, I sway on the spot and continue my head shaking.

.

"Who is she?" I ask at a whisper, almost right into the Bar Manager's ear, like a sleazebag.

"What can I say . . . ," she says with a knowing look on her face. "We can try to work it out."

"Then let's do it."

She holds up three slim unmanicured fingers and racks her brain.

"I think Graham is three score years. How old do you think the girl could be? One? One and a half score? She can't be any more than one and three quarters. There's no way. And no younger than one score. Could she? Seven-eighths? No. She must be a full score, at the very least. I'll be damned if she's a teenager. I'd guess she's one and a half, but it's hard to tell. As you can see for yourself, assumptions about age bounce off her face like water from a block of butter."

"That's for sure," I say.

"Graham's daughter is well over thirty and studies in London, we know that. It's not her."

"No."

"As far as we know, Blaise doesn't have any kids, and definitely not any grandkids. He's barely fifty."

"Could she be a stepchild? Katharina's daughter from a previous relationship?"

"No, Katharina has a son. And look how they're behaving. They're not family."

"I noticed that," I say.

The Bar Manager alternates between twirling the espresso tamper in her fingers and weighing it in her hand, right by her belt buckle. Her gaze is fixed somewhere beyond the horizon. I'm waiting for some kind of continuation.

"Like someone said," she says, "war is the most intelligent form of irrationality."

"Did they?"

"Yeah, a hundred years ago . . ."

"That's something to ponder," I say.

"It comes to me when I look at the girl."

"Ah."

"There's something agitating about her; not exactly violent, but instigating, inflammatory."

"Yeah, it makes you think . . ."

"For sure."

"Don't you have anything more concrete?"

"I've found an odd detail," says the Bar Manager.

"Go on."

"It's not often that pretty women have nicknames. Fine women have names like Jasmine, Caroline, Cameron, Mia, Billy, Cindy, Flannery, Mira. But this one has a nickname."

"Oh?"

"They call her Zloty. She has another name, but people call her Zloty."

"You're kidding."

"No, that's what I've heard."

"But who is she?"

"One thing at a time. Behave yourself, now."

•

The Bar Manager winks at me as she says, "Behave yourself, now." It's a bit much. She needs to calm down. She can't throw that kind of suggestion around. I grab a rag I have no use for. I glance at the crumber. Should I go to the kitchen? Should I top up the Stravecchio? A slight dizziness strikes me. Or maybe it's not dizziness: it feels more like a jolt, some kind of glitch in my attention span; a second or two fold in on themselves and disappear, and I experience a moment of confusion. My field of vision goes milky. Then I'm back, and my years-long routine of waiting kicks in. The Pig doesn't need to give me a sign when he's ready to order; he doesn't have to signal. I know when the Pig is ready. I can feel it. I head over to his table. With his back to me, he starts to dictate into thin air: he knows I'm there.

"We'll take two bottles of the usual, not one; more mineral water; and perhaps you would like to start?" The Pig turns to the Child Lady.

The Child Lady stares at the menu, shakes her head, and passes her turn, the wrong way, to the right, where Blaise is sitting.

"It's a bit early for kid, isn't it?" Blaise says, smiling broadly as he glances around. "I'll take the snails. Give me a couple extra and that'll do."

"Of course," I say.

"I'm always surprised by how filling snails are."

Blaise might have had his hair done right before he came here. Goodness me. He hasn't been threaded at the edge of his beard, has he? No, such a tasteful man would never do that. That's the kind of thing they do in the Middle East. I'm assuming his beard line is naturally strong and well-defined. Now he changes his mind, as he often does.

"Are they really herbs from the Nordmarka forest on the plaice?" he asks, looking at me with eager longing for a concise answer.

"Absolutely," I say, meeting his steady gaze with an absence of doubt concerning the herb question.

"Then I'll try the plaice instead."

"The plaice is an excellent choice."

"I can never get the hang of snail tongs, anyway."

The Pig nods appreciatively, I'm close to saying, but it isn't appreciation for Blaise in his nod—more a kind of confirmation that the choreography of the ordering is going well, despite Blaise's dithering. Now he directs our attention back to the Child Lady, who is still staring at the menu. I hold a small, spade-shaped hand in the air by her face. She could have turned around and gagged on it. With a gentle plop she closes the menu and stares straight ahead, the way she did before the quadruple espresso, with water hazing her eyes.

"Could you fry up a selection of mushrooms? But no oyster mushrooms," she says, her voice sounding completely croaky.

There's a slight rise in the floor, in the mosaic, by the entrance to the rotunda—which isn't actually a rotunda, but which we call one anyway—and I've unintentionally placed my right foot on that rise, which means that I have a slight, awkward forward lean as I give her a nod which conveys certainty, despite the nodding ban.

"The kitchen will take care of it."

I pull back my leg and move my still spade-shaped hand towards the Pig's face.

"I'll take the tartare, but with minimal grape-seed oil, as you know."

"Wonderful," I say, gathering in the menus in a clockwise direction.

·

The chef gets to work like an autist, immediately chopping and frying mushrooms and topping it with a quick flambé. Once he has arranged the mushrooms, the plaice, and the tartare on plates bearing the restaurant emblem, I take the mushrooms and the tartare on my right arm, balance the plaice on my left, and go out and place the mushrooms in front of the Child Lady, the tartare in front of the Pig, and the plaice in front of the inebriated actor at table nine. Blaise stares at me in bewilderment. The Pig makes a strange movement with his hand but doesn't say anything. No one touches their food. The table is completely silent. I draw it out, let the silence become piercing, before I take the fish away from the drunk actor, who actually ordered the confit duck thigh, take the plaice back to table ten, and let it sink down in front of the eyes of the thoroughly maintained Blaise. I hold my slightly stooped position for a few seconds without looking at anyone before I snatch back my hand and stand up with a slight groan, as though to put an end to it. I'm a tall man, impressive to look at, so I've heard, slightly stiff, well built, and so self-confident that I can barely stand upright. I've got wiry facial hair, a mustache. Once, someone told me that I look a bit like Daniel Plainview. I took that to heart. But it's a half-truth. The doggedness might be true. The inflexible stoop might be true. But Plainview is more durable than I am. He looks more outdoorsy. I've got more of a café vibe. Where he's determined and vengeful, I'm more service-oriented and jumpy.

NIEPOORT

THE TALK IS FLOWING NICELY AROUND THE PIG'S
table now. It seems as though they've forgotten my serving blunder. I'm supposed to have a comfortable degree of invisibility: it's
in the job description; it comes naturally to me. I'm not meant to
push myself into the foreground. I glance at the Pig. He's the gentle
type. But he's also a businessman; that can never be forgotten. In a
way, he's always negotiating. With charm and tact, he builds relationships so that he can capitalize on them. I've never understood
negotiating. Isn't it just about discussing your way to the best possible terms for yourself? Advanced haggling, in other words? That's
a primitive thing to be doing. It would never occur to me to ask
for a lower price for something, even if the price was unreasonable. If a seller is brazen enough to be asking for that much, well,
he should get it. I'd rather work a bit more to make up for my loss.
I'm not going to be the one fishing for a reduction. No, haggling
has no place in my culture; we pay full price here.

The Pig gets up. Is he going downstairs to the toilet? No, ugh, he's coming towards me. I fold the napkins as quickly as I can without being sloppy. What does he want now? There are two older women sitting just behind me, whispering away so quietly and feebly that it sounds like whistling. They wheeze a steady stream of half-truths to one another, and one of them is making such sharp *s* sounds that it's like a scalpel slicing my eardrums every time she says "mess" or "west side."

"Excuse me, can I ask you something?" the Pig says gently.

"How can I help?"

"There's something I've been thinking about," says the Pig. "That Tom Sellers character, who often sits at the neighboring table: Do you know him? Isn't he some kind of connoisseur?"

"Could you excuse me for two seconds?" I say, scowling wildly over the heads of the lunch guests. And there, as though on cue, with a comic's timing, the widow of deceased accountant Knipschild gives me a slight wave, indicating that she wants to settle up.

"No, listen here, there's something I want to say," the Pig says.

"Graham, I'm so sorry, could it wait a moment?" I'm squirming like an adder. "I have to see to Widow Knipschild. She's in a hurry. You know: age."

Age? What am I saying? What is happening?

"Not to worry," says the Pig, giving me an utterly bourgeois smile, with the proviso that anything can be called bourgeois in this country. Even the slightest hint of deviation from the intended tone is picked up by us highly sensitives. It may be unfair to call the Pig sly, but I can detect a hint of slyness in him now. What does he mean by "Not to worry"?

Sellers? What does he want from Sellers?

Widow Knipschild is sitting, as she often does, with a book to the side of her plate. She reads page after page. Suddenly, two well-tended hands appear, take hold of the plate, and move it. Her eyes remain fixed on the book; from her angle all she can see are the hands coming in from the side of her field of vision. The hands take things away. They reach for the glasses and napkin. Those hands are mine. It's me. I make objects and food come and go without being noticed myself.

"I'll be back with the bill in a moment, Mrs. Knipschild," I say.

Widow Knipschild has had the foie gras. She has the foie gras quite often. She might even order two courses. First a terrine, then some fried foie gras. She has apple with it, and that apple should have star anise on it. It can even have a bit of caramel. And before you know it, the goose's liver has been washed down with a fortified wine from the pressed grapes of the steep, narrow Douro Valley, and it should say "Port" on the label. If it doesn't say "Port," then these drops are not suitable for washing down the liver of the goose. Not for Widow Knipschild.

She's like a razor, or should I say a Shun knife, when it comes to cutting through the culinary, but using bank cards and payment terminals are not her strong point. The chip is upside down, the strip is worn; the code is forgotten; her bluish, witchlike fingers have to rifle through her purse, where she keeps a handwritten note of her codes—and which are, she claims, also written in code. It gives me time to scan the restaurant, and because of my intimate knowledge of distances and placings here, I know that a glance roughly 110 degrees to the left will give me the opportunity to study the Child Lady in three-quarter profile from behind. As in, I want to be able to study her without her seeing me. From this angle, Blaise suddenly looks like the Child Lady. Maybe it's because I'm straining my eyes. Now both of them resemble the Pig. It's like a magic mirror. The Child Lady is abstract now. I blink. They're joking at the table. The Pig's laughter is loud and ringing, and it always drowns out the others; it sticks out and produces more laughter; it's a kind of laughter which breeds laughter and keeps the collective laughter balls in the air a little longer. Blaise Engelbert has the rougher, more booming type of laugh that members of the social elite often do. His howls of laughter are like the columns beneath the Pig's architrave, if I can put it like that.

The internet is slow today: Widow Knipschild waits on the line. She uses the time to claw about in her pillbox. Out pops a pill, then another one. She takes a tablet. What's that tablet for? Or possibly against?

"Excuse me?"

Her head trembles faintly as she looks up at me. The payment goes through.

"Couldn't I have another glass of Niepoort?"

Knipschild has the metallic clang which often takes over elderly ladies' vocal cords.

"Of course," I say. And this is a bit unfortunate, but her previous glass was actually the last of the Niepoort. In other words, I'll have to go down to the cellar. Why? Because the short-haired, anemic Vanessa, who has less seniority than I do, and who usually goes to the cellar if it's needed, is out for a while. Out for a while? An errand, the Maître d' said. She's having her hair cut. I asked again. Hair cut? When did the waiters start getting their hair cut during working hours? This is a European restaurant, not a beauty salon. You come presentable, you leave presentable. Never bother the colleagues with your upkeep. Of all things, the Maître d' is generous about Vanessa cutting her hair. The whitest tablecloths get dirty first, he says. I'll have to go down to the cellar.

THE CELLAR

THE GOODS CELLAR BENEATH THE HILLS IS WHERE we store all our pillages; everything has to go down there. Access to the cellar is from the street, something which is fairly unusual in Oslo, but which you see quite often in New York, for example, where things are always being heaved down to the cellars beneath buildings through hatches in the street. These access points are ideally holes in the ground, right in front of the building—the restaurant, the nail bar, or whatever it is—with a trapdoor over the top, and it seems really tricky to take the goods down there, but it's the only place where there's room; they don't have any choice.

Down in the goods cellar there is an intricate shelving system. I don't have much business in the cellar. I've never been to the very end of it, the deepest part. I'm not usually the one to fetch things from down here, but I've been in the area closest to the stairs and peered in. I've seen how the shelving system vanishes into the darkness. The chef has explained in a mumble that the walkway splits in two farther ahead, in a fork. The walls are curved, and the shelving system, which consists of both open and closed shelves as well as small drawers in two layers, adapts to these curves. There are also a number of cupboards placed randomly on top of and next to one another, and cabinets with beveled fronts that are divided into smaller cupboards. These give more of an impression of being some kind of electric panels than cabinets as such. Parts of the shelves—or is it the wall?—are covered in metal plates which would likely have been made from titanium or magnesium on a space station, but which are possibly sheet metal or tin down here. Yes, the incalculable level of detail seems more like some kind of elongated cockpit than a storeroom, workshop, or garage. The way they've utilized the space is unbelievable. The abundance of surfaces, platforms, and spaces always means a new abundance of surfaces, platforms, and spaces. You can practically experience a "fractal" solution and richness of detail. It's hard to describe, but the rounded walls, which would otherwise have been problematic for conventional, straight shelving systems, are handled by this ingenious storage architecture so that the shelves actually provide more storage space than if they had been straight. And they say—it's said, they allege, it's claimed—that this system, and this incredible use of space, continues all the way to the end of the cellar, but I haven't personally been there, to the end, like I said. I haven't even seen the infamous fork.

The shelving system is old. They say that parts of it have been here since the beginning. Yes, they say that Benjamin Hill, the founder himself, built the shelves just before his clothing business went bust. That seems likely. The drawers and small cabinets are ideal for haberdashery, buttons, spools, combs, and hardware, needles, screws, hangers, knobs, pins, and so on. They say that Hill hid down there in shame between drinking sprees and dizzying financial losses at the poker table; it was down there that he took himself when everything else seemed impossible. This isn't just drawn out of thin air; it's written that Hill was an apprentice with his uncle's carpentry firm in Windsor around 1830, half a decade before the charmer and dandy in him emerged and drove him to the exclusive and frivolous environments of the capital. And from there, through various detours, to Oslo. Or Kristiania, as the city was known at the time. Regardless, this goddamn shelving system—which, in truth, is a composite structure from many different epochs, and has had to be repaired, improved, and patched up at regular intervals since Benjamin Hill's original structure went up—is, as I've mentioned, both intricate and innovative; and it works well enough that it hasn't needed to be changed while The Hills has been home to the sale of either attire or the edible. It's as though, with all the small repairs, improvements, and complications, the "resolution" of the entire structure is higher, almost as though the years of use and expansion have made it organic. The shelving system has *grown*; it's crackled and folded into itself through the shifts between use, wear, and repair, use, improvement, and more wear. If you can imagine some kind of shelving version of the sticker-covered walls up in the restaurant, it's like that. Layer on layer. Intention on intention. Use over use.

•

Luckily, the Niepoort is close to the stairs. I need to take only a few steps along the left-hand row of shelves to find a wide, aged, extendable drawer-like shelf of steel. It's forged, heavy as lead, moves easily on well-functioning runners, and has some kind of velour padding inside. The drawer is full of Niepoort, Ruby, Tawny, Colheita, and so on. And some Tokaji, oddly enough. Oh, they're roomy, these drawers. I take out two Niepoorts, but as I try to close the drawer by giving it a hard shove with my hip, I manage to trap my left hand something awful. What do you call the edge of your hand, or the back of the hand right down by the lower side of the little finger, where the back of the hand turns into the palm? What do you call it, by the wrist joint at the bottom? What the hell's that called, the bit between the wrist and the little finger's joint, the karate chop part, the hand knife? Is it the hypothenar muscle? Is that the word I've heard? The bit which gets paralyzed if you hit your elbow, if you give your *nervus ulnaris* a jolt, if you bang your so-called funny bone and experience what the Norwegians call widower's grief, because it's over so quickly, and your little and ring fingers are often paralyzed. That's the part I manage to trap in the heavy, smooth drawer. What can I say? The pain is hellish. I moan loudly and hiss between my teeth, which means I also send a string of drool down onto my nice waiter's jacket. I manage to drop the bottles to the floor without breaking them, press my hand between my thighs, and continue to hiss and splutter, because this is absolutely womb-crushingly painful. I don't dare open my thighs to look. It's impossible to tell whether my hand is crushed, cut, or broken, or what has happened. It hurts so much that it feels like someone is kidding with me. I can't believe it. I try to walk off the pain. I walk and walk, I stagger knock-kneed back and forth between the rows of shelves with my hands clasped between my thighs. I don't go too far down the walkway, because I don't want to go in, I don't under any circumstances want to go *deeper* into this moldy cellar. This gathering place for all sorts of things. I doubt I've cut myself, I rub my hands together, and it doesn't feel wet, it doesn't feel like there's any blood. I don't want to look. I stand beneath the streets of old Oslo and groan.

I've got a hemorrhage beneath the skin: a blister the size of an unused condom puffs up. It's swelling, and I'm thinking of piercing it, but I'll have to go and see the chef for that; I'm not aware of any medical tools down here. I grab the two bottles of Niepoort in my right hand and clamp the injured left one in the opposite armpit. I'll be damned. I flip the cellar trapdoor (steel) shut with my heel, and it makes a terrible noise as it hits the frame (also steel). That's just how it'll have to be. I go round the corner and in through the back door, into the kitchen.

"Can you poke a hole in this?" I say to the chef, holding up the blister.

"We'll see to that."

"It's really bursting."

"I'll do it with the oyster knife."

At the same time, I hear a "Hello" from the swing doors. It's the Maître d', puffed up, staring. I reply hurriedly:

"Yes?"

"Vanessa needs a hand," says the Maître d'.

"Vanessa's back?"

"Yes, she's back. Hair cut."

"Ah."

"Who looks outside, dreams; who looks inside, awakes."

". . ."

"She needs help. She hasn't served table thirteen before."

"Table thirteen's arrived?" I say.

"Table thirteen has arrived," says the Maître d'.

"Oh no."

PART III

SELLERS AND
HIS GROUP

UGH, TOM SELLERS AND HIS GROUP HAVE PLACED
themselves at table thirteen, their usual table, right by the bar,
two tables away from table ten, where the Pig sits enthroned with
his chosen ones. Table thirteen is also my table. This isn't good.
Sellers has, on par with the Pig but for radically different reasons
(to do with the aforementioned donations), access to The Hills as
his own "parlor." Sellers and his followers usually come at night,
when the noise levels are slightly higher and the morals a little
lower, but they're here now, Sellers, Bratland, and Raymond, at
1:47, right in the middle of the day.

He never makes a fuss per se, Sellers. He's a so-called *gessæl*,
as they say in the countryside; a scamp, but a cultured one. *Gesell*,
they used to call them in the olden days. When the apprentices
began their roving, particularly to Germany in the seventeenth
and eighteenth centuries, the term "wandering *Gesell*" developed

something odious about it, meaning vagrant or vagabond. Strictly speaking, Sellers is fairly well rooted, but he possesses that stray, vagabond-esque aura which characterizes certain people, perhaps fewer and fewer, particularly here in the organized north. He's a rascal. The image of cultivated scamp that he radiates makes him irresistible to many. Maybe not irresistible but appealing. Or maybe not appealing in the sense of being attractive, or magnetic, but of being desirable to aspiring scamps. The scamp in Sellers gives him an authority in certain environments. He has an aged scamp's face. Sellers has that thick, leathery George Clooney skin on his face, but he's more worn, grayer, and without Clooney's fortunate bone structure. He's not an ugly Clooney: he's got Clooney's skin stretched over a bigger skull. Clooney's skin smoke-clogged, boozed up, and stretched over a scamp's cranium. His hair is starting to turn gray. He looks like a Picabia who's had a bad night's sleep. He gives a mousy impression, even if he is fundamentally "robust."

Hence Sellers doesn't radiate the type of upkeep which otherwise characterizes the clientele at The Hills. He's a handsome man, I want to say that. A bit threadbare and rough, but tranquil. No nerve face. He looks intelligent, and that gives his shabbiness bite. He's rustily al dente. And then there's the effect of the alcohol. Some people's drunkenness is helpless or foolish. Sellers's drunkenness is perceived as intended and challenging. One can interpret Sellers's drunkenness as a critique of other people's sobriety. He *snuggles* when a situation gets tight. Sellers is someone who likes devilry. Fun is produced all around him. He's almost impossible to knock off his perch. Sellers looks uncomfortable. He looks double. He isn't simple. Sellers is complex. There's no understanding him. Is he an enigma? He probably is. What does he *want*? you ask yourself. What does he do?

"Never will I work, O torrents of flame!" Was that Rimbaud? Sellers doesn't do much. But he keeps on. There are plenty of stories about him. The General Manager, M. Hill, who, on her part, is very obliging to Sellers and his group (donations), claims, via the Bar Manager, that Sellers and his friends, without contributing a thing, relate to a *certain* story precisely because of this intended uselessness, a *certain* historical trend, a tradition which puts infantile nonsense above all else. Sellers has never been part of any historical trend, the Maître d' protests—rather the opposite—but the General Manager, via the Bar Manager, claims that Sellers's endless stream of nonsense actively reflects certain features of the twentieth century's cultural history. The Maître d' says that that is being too generous, he isn't impressed; but the General Manager stands her ground. Taking pride in her profession, as she does, she wants there to be a trace of this cultural history at The Hills, the family business, which, strictly speaking, there already is, in the form of the stickers and all the art, but that's not enough for the General Manager. She wants the story to continue to play out, not to go on or evolve, but to be repeated indefinitely, so that everything that wasn't ridiculed, distracted, and mocked fully during the first round, from 1914 onwards, can be ridiculed and derailed again

and again in the same way. The great ridiculing which began in
the early twentieth century, in The Hills's golden days, was never
completed, according to General Manager M. Hill, via the Bar
Manager; it'll never be completed, and that means a cut through
time is needed, so that the positions begun but never finished, and
the ridiculing, which are the only positions of value, can be picked
up anew and repeated, played out again and again. These are positions which will always be misunderstood, and which therefore
always have to be repeated, so that the misunderstanding is maintained forever, since misunderstandings are often more effective
here and now than as history. The Hills is one of the few places
where there is room for that. That's what the General Manager
says, pompously.

•

Sellers is dour: he's no picnic, that's true, but that in itself doesn't
make him heir to the dadaist throne or anything, says the Maître d'.
Sellers, Raymond, and Bratland carry on with their tenacious,
aimless, stagnant nonsense, but from there to the Pantheon is quite
some distance, the Maître d' insists irritably. The beach that's said
to be beneath the cobblestones—well, Sellers and his colleagues
usually find it at the bottom of a bottle, the General Manager says.
But being drunk and disgusting isn't an art form, the Maître d'
protests; no, on the contrary. The bitter attacks that Sellers and his
group direct at everyone around them are weak, a bit schmuckish.

The only thing they've worked out, if you ask the Maître d', if we're following the General Manager's line of thought via the Bar Manager, is the classic question of whether they should have fun in the here and now, in life as such, or save the unleashing of desire until after the "revolution." Since we're no longer in a position to see "revolution" on the horizon, Sellers, Bratland, and Raymond have fun—*fun*—right here and now. They've long known, the General Manager argues, that we're moving about in a representation; a social, political, economic, existential representation, which, as an increasing number realize, has become a sheer parody of what was once an "existence"; the situation, the conditions, have moved so far past being a joke, a pure jest, that all suitable responses have stopped being suitable. Mockery is the only thing left. Sellers once said to her, the General Manager claims, that what he is trying to do is prevent the day from being nothing more than twenty-four hours of wasted time. Well, even the Maître d' agrees with that. But that's where the agreement comes to an end.

It might look like Sellers is smoking in here, but he isn't. The smoking ban came into force years ago, and even the avant-gardist smokes outside now. Sellers "acts" like he's smoking; he looks like some kind of '20s photo, or, to be more precise: he looks like a photo from 1923. I look like a photo from 1890, if it weren't for the Child Lady sitting right behind me being wildly contemporary. The Pig looks like a photo from 1984. Sellers's slender friend Bratland looks like a gnome. His face is at once young and old.

I've never liked this Bratland. Eyes close together. I have quite a liking for Sellers and Raymond, despite all the nonsense, but I can do without Bratland. I'm jumpy around Sellers, but he is dashing. Bratland is foul. He always has a foul expression on his face. A snakelike smile. Dead, mackerel eyes. Always a remark. Bratland will be bald in three seconds. He's not much to look at. To be more precise, and keep the mood in the early twentieth century: he actually looks like Jacques Vaché. He's got the ratty, Conan O'Brien–like face of Vaché placed on the high shoulders of Bernie Sanders. And with bad teeth.

If an obscure name is mentioned around table thirteen, the otherwise talkative Bratland goes quiet. Then he goes to the toilet while Sellers and Raymond continue to talk, and when he comes back, he suddenly has plenty to contribute. He's been trawling the internet from the toilet seat; he's been reading up. A crowd-sourced genius emerges from the bathroom. He always uses the internet to cover over his grotesque incompetence. Raymond, the great beluga of a third man in Sellers's group, is the opposite. He looks like a hobo with a greasy fringe. His face is a mask of hairy old leather with two holes and a ravine, but what comes from this ravine, his ravine of a mouth, is pure gold. Raymond has internalized knowledge; he isn't a toilet-porcelain dean like Bratland. Raymond has a scar under his mouth which makes him look slightly affected, slightly sore, as though his chin is constantly rippling with tears. Raymond has a sweaty charisma and is well liked. He is extremely capable. I don't know what a genius looks like, but I can recognize one when I see it. He's only ever addressed as Raymond and has always gone by that one name, despite the fact that he is the golden child, while Bratland, paradoxically, is the one with many names. "Sir Hiss" is one of them, the result of his serpentine snaking around Sellers. Bratland once sold a flat well below the valuation and became known as "the Valuation Man" afterwards. "Bucket" is from the day they went berry picking, when Sellers tricked him into *only* picking unripe fruit. "What have you got in your bucket?" people kept asking him nonstop. On a trip to Warsaw, Bratland went a bit far in dishing out his local knowledge—he studied there six months during the '80s—and became known as "the Polack" the following autumn. And, as Sellers's partner in Düsseldorf, after shouting "*Genug!*" at a shoe-shine boy who had shined his new leather shoes too hard, he became known as "Genug." That's the name used most often, after Bratland, particularly by Raymond. He says "Genug" every time he should say "Bratland."

THE SITUATION

HAVE THE FESTIVITIES GONE FULL CIRCLE? SELLERS and company are slow in their movements. They're by no means loud or screeching, the way people usually are after, say, a liquid lunch; instead, they seem to be in the *slump* you experience when the party has gone on for almost twenty-four hours, when the party has become a test of endurance, a marathon, some kind of job. Sellers's group seems more concentrated than festive. They're baby animals on their first day. Sellers's hand gestures are sluggish and his gaze is slow. I hold the hand with the blister behind my back and come to the aid of the newly hired, short-haired Vanessa as she wanders about with the stack of menus clutched to her chest. I know Sellers. Or know and know—I know him as well as I know all the other regulars here. I've been seeing him for years. He's been seeing me for years. I know plenty about him. He knows nothing about me.

"Would you like to see the menu?"

Tom Sellers rubs his thighs. He rubs his avant-garde thighs.

It's hard to tell whether he's an alcoholic as such, but that rubbing could seem addict-esque. A bit needy. He's always drunk. They decide on a round of Birra Morettis; all but Bratland, aka the Polack, aka Bucket, aka Genug, who wants white wine.

"The house white?" I ask.

"No."

"Would you like to see the wine menu?"

"Rather not."

"I see."

"You don't have a Californan chardonnay? Californian."

"Of course."

"Then I'll have a huge glass of that."

"Anything to eat?"

There's something about keeping up the formalities, even with boisterous types like Sellers and his group. We all know that they're going to eat, but we also know that it's *comme il faut* to ask rather than assume, so I take the job of asking, staring, and waiting. I can do that. The exchange of glances ends with a nod from Sellers; I take my hand and my blister over to the bar, where I find the Morettis, previously brewed in Udine but now owned by Heineken—isn't that right?—plus the chardonnay, which has been grown, picked, and crushed in sun-drenched California. My blister throbs and stings. I need to finish serving the drinks before the chef and I get to work with the oyster knife. Puncturing stuff, poking holes, penetrating, is never on top of my list. But what are the alternatives? The blister is about to pop.

•

Sellers starts singing quietly:

> *E ricomincerà*
> *Come da un rendez-vous*

Many years ago, we had a jukebox here, just like Cuneo in ugly Hamburg, which played Paolo Conte and other Italian classics with plenty of echo. *Gli impermeabili*, and so on. I think Sellers misses it.

"Please, Sellers," Bratland says.

"Keep out of it, Genug," says Raymond.

The atmosphere around the three is a strange mix of refreshing and unpleasant. Can you imagine a smell that's both fresh and rotten? Once, I had to swap a bunch of lilies which had gone off in their vase. Our florist had let it happen. They didn't smell of lilies anymore; they smelled like crap. The strange thing was that the lilies were still in bloom, but their stalks had withered. A sweet smell of decay mixed with the fragrance of the flowers. Lilies have a truly disturbing scent, especially if you don't cut off the small stamen, or whatever it is that's inside the flower; that's what stinks. Our florist annoys me. He lets that happen sometimes. No one from Sellers's group looks up when I serve them their beverages. I turn my left hand inwards, like a claw, to avoid showing the blister. He's an observant guy, Sellers. Not rude, but sometimes he'll comment on small things that embarrass you. What am I saying? They embarrass *me*. I can't speak for others. He's the intelligent type, someone who always sees more than he says.

I don't want any questions about it: I hide the blister. It was unfortunate that it happened. It was no one's fault. I can't point the finger at Widow Knipschild for sending me down to the cellar. Widow Knipschild! Damn it. I glance over to her table, and there she is with an empty glass, looking straight at me. Ugh, her old eyes are staring, her colorless eyeballs searching me and asking, yes, wondering what happened to her Niepoort and why I'm prioritizing these youngish (really middle-aged) woozy men. Widow Knipschild's poor eyes. Just imagine everything they've seen. Imagine all the tears that have spilled from them. They've had their fill, those eyes, throughout their long lives, of staring and crying. And here they are, let down again. The last thing her tired eyes need is to register yet another disappointment. The opposite of "opening your chest" seems to be happening to me now: I can feel my chest contracting. My breathing becomes shallow. It often does when I've got too much on my plate. Widow Knipschild is sitting there with her eyeballs; she even lifts a bony hand into the air to catch my attention. Her hand shakes so slowly that it looks like she's waving. And as though that waving, bony hand weren't enough, the Pig also turns his head and nods to me. What does he want now? What does he want, this Pig, who has everything? I signal that I'll be with him in two seconds. Vanessa is still circling Sellers's table. The blister is pulsing. I hurry into the kitchen.

•

"Can you pop it?"

"What?"

"The blister."

"Let's see."

The chef takes my wrist in an excessively hard grip and breathes a long, slow breath through his squashed nose. He studies my hand the way a blacksmith would study another blacksmith's work, for example, or the way a sushi chef would study a piece of fish by turning it and peering at it from different angles. I don't know why he wants to seem so "professional"; he's a chef, not a surgeon. To him, to whom God gives office, He gives also understanding. But the chef's office isn't the puncturing of blisters. He takes the oyster knife from the magnetic strip—it's mounted beneath the bench, not above it—and presses down firmly into the blister. The stream of blood must be thinner than a strand of hair. Like an acupuncture needle, inexplicably thin. I don't think the chef sees it to begin with; his eyes aren't the best. The squirt has time to hit the chest of his worn, white chef's jacket before moving upwards, across his collar, up his neck, towards his face. Suddenly it's on his cheek. Now he reacts. Maybe he's equipped with particularly sensitive nerve endings on the skin beneath his eyes. "*Eeeeiii,*" he bellows in disgust, with some kind of *euhhh/aaah* sound, meaning his bellow becomes an odd mix of a word and a shout, a noise with no specific meaning, almost like retching, a sound produced by the body when language falls away. He grimaces, or smiles, and it looks like he has a tear of blood on his cheek, which he quickly wipes away with the arm of his jacket. He wraps one of the tea towels around my hand before he presses on the blister and empties the blood into the linen.

The question is how loud his shout was. Did I hear a moment's pause in the clink of cutlery and buzz of voices from out in the restaurant? It was a bizarre sound he produced, the chef. A shout and a retching sound which was also like a bleat from the mouth of a sheep. Muzzle. The snout of a sheep? That's how he bleated. Did they hear it? I try to sigh but can't get the air all the way in, and I produce a strained hiss instead of the deep housewife's sigh I wanted to make. The blister is empty and has become a pale flap of skin instead of a potent, full blister.

"What do we do now?" I say.

"You'll have to put gauze on it; otherwise you'll tear the skin."

"Do we have any gauze?"

"Maybe a bit. In the wardrobe."

I have to get going. The Pig is waiting, Widow Knipschild's glass is still empty. She needs her Niepoort. She'll get so much Niepoort. And the Pig: Does he want to see the dessert menu, or does he want to tease and agitate me with abstract questions about Sellers and rare works of art? I squeeze past the chef, go over to the old yellow medicine cabinet in the wardrobe, and apply a double compress over the skin flap. I'm terrible at applying compresses; it ends up lopsided and loose. I wrap what little gauze there is around my hand. It really is an amateurish attempt. What kind of provocation is he up to, the Pig? With the Niepoort in my good hand, I go out through the swing doors, back into the restaurant, back to the guests. The Pig turns to me—ugh. He holds my gaze. The Child Lady also looks up. Ugh. Widow Knipschild stares at me with those gray eyeballs, waiting, hoping for the bottle of Niepoort. I go to her first. I hold the Niepoort high, almost level with my breastbone, so that there's no doubt in Widow Knipschild's mind what is about to happen.

It's generous, the serving I give her. I don't stop. I fill it to the brim.

"Oh, thank you, thank you," she says.

Then the Pig.

"You're busy?" he says.

I recognize it well, around my right eye, the tension. I don't know what my right eye has to do with my emotional state, but it's always around my right eye that it appears. "It" appears. What does? Distaste. Anxiety. *Tension.*

"How was the food?" I ask.

"Wonderful," says the Pig.

"And the mushrooms did the job?" I say to the Child Lady. She giggles. "That depends which job they were supposed to do." Blaise chuckles. Which job were the mushrooms supposed to do? Who knows. They were supposed to do the mushroom job, I guess. I will not try to be funny now. Unhappiness makes reliable consumers, Edgar often says. That also applies to the Child Lady.

She smiles a childlike smile, but she's not fooling me. How many squadrons of riot police are needed for the Child Lady to smile like a child? I make use of my only defense, the standard phrases.

"Can I tempt you with anything sweet?"

My left hand is firmly behind my back to avoid waving the gauze bandage in the guests' faces. A compress placed over a wound isn't exactly what you want to see while you're tucking into char, a tart, or bouillabaisse. The only problem is that my back is turned to the watchful Sellers and company while I talk to the Pig: my hand is on show, so to speak; it's illuminated no matter which way I turn. I can almost feel Sellers and his group's eyes burning on the compress and the loose flap beneath it while I try to tend to the Pig. Sellers is so conflict oriented. I mean, not in a persistent, crude way, but in the intelligent double or triple way which, I want to say, is worse than one single, inappropriate, simple, embarrassing outburst. I turn to him.

"Everything OK out in the kitchen?" Sellers says ambiguously.

"Oh yes."

"Just let us know if you need any help."

"That won't be necessary," I say.

"Oh, well," says Sellers. "Just let us know."

"Anything else to drink?" I ask.

"Have you lost weight?"

Sometimes, as I'm serving or taking orders, I become aware of my own stooping. My stoop. There are no extenuating circumstances around being stooped, but there can, seen from a particular angle, be something about stooping which fits well with being a waiter. There's plenty of leaning forward in this job. I'm bent over Sellers's table right now. It might not look completely crazy for a waiter, but we're talking about a serious stoop here. I stoop more when the situation weighs.

"I've been the same weight since I was nineteen," I say.

"Good age. Nineteen. The evenings. The oomph," Sellers says ambiguously.

It's just a case of getting away. I've signaled that Vanessa should take the dessert and coffee orders from the Pig's table. What will it be? Vanessa manages to mess it up. She can't keep track of a single cortado, a double espresso, a double cortado, and a single americano. She has to ask again. Were both cortados doubles? No, just the one. And the americanos? Single? Yes. And a double espresso, no? "This shouldn't be so difficult," says Blaise. And he says it in a slightly prissy manner. He snaps slightly; there's a sting to what he says. A sting which is heard a bit too far away. The observant Sellers and his table are *very* sensitive to snapping and prissiness. They might be endlessly indifferent to their own appearance, to the unease they consistently bring with them, but other people's snapping, stinging—particularly if it is directed "downwards, from above," as they say—well, that's going to be noticed. A snap of the kind Blaise serves to Vanessa is seen as crude by Sellers and his group, I know that. I know them well. Blaise is, as described, particularly well maintained. Crudeness becomes proportionally cruder depending on how well groomed the supplier of the crudeness is. As a result, the crudeness he casts out becomes utterly piggish in Sellers's and Bratland's ears. There will be consequences, I fear.

Sellers would never attack with anything but his vocabulary. Tricks and cons in an emergency. He waves Vanessa over and calmly reels off what he wants. Vanessa nods despairingly. It's a lot to remember. She goes to the bar and immediately returns with a number of coffees, plus a stack of hors d'oeuvres on a serving tray. It almost seems like she won't be able to carry it. She approaches Sellers first and puts down two of the coffees, but Sellers corrects her and she takes them back, not without effort, then carries the whole overfilled tray to the Pig's table and sets them out, one by one, plus a total of seven bowls of fennel salami; the Pig's company is silent while she works. And once the slightly thrall-looking Vanessa is finished, there are nine double americanos and one Turkish coffee on table ten, in addition to all the salami. Vanessa studies the table. What has she done?

"Johansen!" Sellers shouts.

The playing stops.

"*Schweigt stille, plaudert nicht!*"

Johansen fires up Bach's Coffee Cantata.

·

No blows are dealt, of course, but there are ripples on the water. Blaise gets up and goes over to Sellers's table. Bratland, confrontational as he is, gets up to meet Blaise. They stand there, uneasily close to one another. Bratland is a good ten centimeters shorter than Blaise, Blaise is seven miles ahead when it comes to attire.

"Is this your coffee order?" says Blaise.

"I order coffee from time to time," says Bratland.

"Is it his?" Blaise points to Sellers.

"What's wrong with coffee?" says Bratland.

"What?"

"The tycoon's out strolling?"

"What's going on?" says Blaise.

"Manners. They apply to you, too. You're in a restaurant."

"Come again?"

Blaise holds out his arms and glances around as though searching for confirmation of the absurdities coming out of Bratland. He doesn't get a thing. Perplexed, Vanessa begins to move coffees and fennel salami from the Pig's table back to Sellers's. The Maître d' and I approach the two parties from different directions; he asks them to pull themselves together. Bratland doesn't care about that, but Blaise yields, gentleman that he is. He takes a step back. I place a hand between Bratland's shoulders to pacify him, but Bratland twists like a teenager.

"Shame!" he says, pointing a finger at Blaise.

The Maître d' takes Blaise by the upper arm and places his other hand on the back of his polished neck. He steers the fragrant man back to the Pig's table. Will Bratland give in now? Ack, he grabs a piece of salami from one of the bowls of hors d'oeuvres.

But before he has time to throw it at Blaise or the Child Lady, or eat it, or do whatever it is he's planning to do, Sellers swats his hand, making him drop it. I shout a firm "Hey!" The fennel salami flies in a gentle arc, straight into the glass of the lovely little Isa Genzken assemblage hanging to the right of table fifteen before falling behind the almost monstrous radiator which stands there with its countless layers of peeling glossy varnish. The Maître d' reacts strongly, with a jolt, a spasm.

"Watch the Genzken!" he says, pointing firmly at the artwork.

The fennel salami leaves a greasy mark on the glass. Sellers squints. He's enjoying this. It looks like he's trying to focus on the grease on the Genzken. He's trying to get the fat in focus, to take it in.

NEZ

"YOU CLEAN THE GENZKEN," THE MAÎTRE D' SAYS,
his voice thick.

I go straight into the kitchen to get the spray. The chef looks
up at me from his flambéing. He probably heard the commotion
out there, but doesn't ask; he never asks. He has an ability, the chef,
to know exactly what's going on in the restaurant without being
there himself. And while I'm wiping, the Pig comes over and asks
whether the picture is OK. Sure, it's fine. It's just grease. And then
he's at it again. He wants to talk. It was a bit unfortunate, he says,
this episode. Because it was Sellers he wanted me to introduce him
to. It so happens that Blaise has come across an artwork they need
someone with competence to look at. And it should be someone
who—how to put it? says the Pig. Someone who will give it a look
under the table. Sellers is competent, so they've heard. That may
be, I say dismissively. I don't want to run this through restaurant
management, says the Pig. It would be best if you, being a waiter,

could introduce me to Sellers, says the Pig. Completely without obligation.

I decline. It's way beyond my scope, I say. I don't want to get mixed up in this. Take it up with the General Manager (M. Hill). But you don't understand, says the Pig. Blaise has a real gem at his place—yes, he has one of Hans Holbein the Younger's small portrait sketches there: not one of the most famous; a small, bleak one, but it's a Holbein all the same; one of the Tudor drawings, no more, no less—and the Pig needs to get a conversation about it under way, with someone suitably discreet. Something the Pig assumes Sellers is. Blaise is thinking about donating it. No thanks, I say again. Holbein? No, no. I say it straight: You'll have to do that yourself, Graham. I don't want to get mixed up in this. But I need an introduction, says the Pig. The Pig is old-school: he demands an introduction. Then you'll have to introduce yourself, I say, surprised by my own directness.

With that, the Pig leaves. Blaise struts off through the curtain with market liberal steps. The Child Lady remains. I'm still double-checking that the Genzken is grease-free. The Maître d' is in the middle of the room. He has paused, as rigid as a stone. The Maître d's face—which, even to begin with, has that drinker's glow, that unhealthy hue—has turned an even deeper shade after what just occurred. I think the Child Lady should leave. She should have the decency to leave the establishment and allow the dust to settle. But instead she hangs around like a bacillus. She moves, that's true, but only to a different table, to one of the smaller marble tops by the entrance. I wish she were gone. I wish she had never stepped her fancy foot in here. How can we push her out?

Sellers looks absent, with a thousand-yard stare, seemingly unaffected by the unpleasantries which just took place. His group orders new rounds of Moretti—all but Bratland, who insists on the dumb California chardonnay. It's gone four, almost half past. Here Edgar comes, holding the curtain to one side for Anna, who slips in beneath his arm, radiantly cheerful, with her sweet child's face in the middle of her head, if I can put it like that. Does she sense the toxic atmosphere? Should I escort her chaste, guiltless soul right back out?

"Hi!" she says to me. Edgar is also in a mood.

"Do your homework, Anna," he says.

Anna pulls out her books with a complete lack of complaint: she starts *immediately*, with no hesitation; it truly is inspiring to see how she buckles down without beating about the bush. All that back-and-forth—what's it good for? I hold the hand with the bandage close to my left thigh.

"Dad says you're good at piano."

"Not at all," I say. "I've never played piano. What homework do you have?"

"Maths."

"What kind of maths?"

"Geometry."

"Oh, that's easy."

"Yeah . . . but the compass wobbles when I try to draw circles. It's loose."

"Let's see."

I catch a slight whiff of pencil case as she pulls it out. The mix of pencil and eraser has the distinct smell of school. So they're still doing it. Pencils and erasers. It won't last. Nothing does. I take the compass; it is fairly slack, and a loose compass joint is, as everyone knows, frustrating. Grotesque, even. A compass is anything but a compass when it's loose.

"I'll ask the chef to tighten it," I say.

The chef nods mutely in the kitchen and tightens the compass screw with the tip of his most expensive Henckels knife before turning back to the careful frying of beef tournedos. I don't smell the chef's cooking anymore, but I know that this dish in particular has an exceptional scent. But God help me if I haven't forgotten to add both the tournedos and the coq au vin to the board of recommendations. I grab a piece of chalk from the bowl behind the spool of butcher's twine. As I walk through the restaurant, Bratland shouts "Rach!" loudly, which means that Old Johansen switches to Rachmaninoff up on the mezzanine, the internal balcony, and Piano Concerto no. 3 it is, Bratland's favorite. I take the Morettis and the chardonnay and let them land, as quickly as three tits on a bird table, beneath the noses of Bratland, Raymond, and Sellers. Then I hand the compass to Anna.

"What's going on?" says Edgar.

"'Going on'?" I raise an eyebrow and try to hold my face steady; I try dragging it in the opposite direction to the downwards pull caused by the strain.

"You look a bit harried."

"We had a slight situation."

"A *situation*?"

"A slight situation."

"I see."

Edgar doesn't have much patience for my noncommunicative tendencies. He shrugs. Anna is busy drawing perfect circles with the newly tightened compass. From the corner of my eye, I can see that the Child Lady has flagged down the inexperienced Vanessa. She spends a while talking to her; it seems like more than an order. What is she planting in Vanessa now? What seeds, which ideas?

"Anna's worked out what she wants to be," says Edgar.

"Oh yeah?" I say. "A geometricist?"

"There's no such thing as a geometricist," says Anna.

"What do you want to be, then?"

"A perfumist."

"A perfumist?"

"Yes."

"There's no such thing as a perfumist," I say.

"I want to work in a perfume shop."

"You want to be a perfume shop employee?"

"Yes."

"That's something different to a perfumist."

"OK, a perfume shop employee, then."

"If there's such a thing as a perfumist, it must be someone who *makes* perfume," I say.

"They're called perfumers," says Edgar.

"Yes, of course."

"Or *nez*."

"*Nez*. French for 'nose.' Someone with a good sense of smell," says Edgar.

"I don't want to be a *nez*," says Anna. "I want to work in a perfume shop."

"Why's that?"

"The people working there are so cheerful."

"That's true," says Edgar. "They are."

"You want to be cheerful," I say.

"Yes," says Anna. "That's what happens when you work in a perfume shop."

"I suppose it is."

Edgar explains that they were in a perfume shop the other day. It had struck him (them) how incredibly positive the woman working there was. She was so unbelievably cheerful, he says, and Anna agrees.

"You should sell something which smells good and makes people glad," says Edgar.

"That's nice." Anna nods.

"We talked about it afterwards," says Edgar, "about how

cheerful and nice she was. Same thing at Anna's orthodontist. The woman behind the counter is so boundlessly positive. You should fit braces to teeth so they become straight and inviting. You should do the job really well and no more, but no less, either. You should be in a position to send people home with straight teeth or smelling nice. And then you could head off at the weekend to the cabin or some other nice place as fast as your feet can carry you. Ideally every weekend. And on top of that, you should focus intensely on holidays and celebrations. Get completely into the Christmas preparations. Decorate without restraint. Master Christmas. Go crazy with Easter eggs and decorative birch twigs when the time comes. I think that's a source of happiness. Seriously."

"What did you buy at the perfume shop?" I ask.

Edgar draws it out.

"Something for a friend."

"Well, what do you know," I say.

"Musk," says Anna.

"Musk?"

I know who all of Edgar's female friends are. He isn't buying musk for any of them, that much is certain. This is interesting. The musk is left hanging in the air alongside everything else that's already hanging in the air. There's so much hanging in the air. Is there ever nothing hanging in the air?

"Who is this friend?"

"One you don't know about."

Anna places one leg of the compass in front of the other and allows it to walk like a thin, stiff-legged fellow across the sheet of paper in her notebook, not dissimilar to the way I trudge around. I've started to trudge with age. If I have to do a U-turn, I take a number of supporting side steps rather than one firm, solid turn.

Sellers waves to me. He isn't any more sober, nor is he more drunk; he's *level*, I suppose you could say. He wants food.

"What do you two want?" I say to Edgar and Anna. "I have to move on."

"I want lasagne," says Anna.

"I'll have the butter sole," says Edgar.

"The butter sole," I repeat.

"Can you add some extra capers?"

"Extra capers on the butter sole."

"It's a bit strange, maybe, but I once had a spoonful of date jelly on the side. Can you arrange that?"

"Date with the butter sole. Of course."

"Date," says Anna.

"Do you want date?"

"No, dates are . . ." She waves her hand in front of her nose and pulls a face.

"Ask him to over-fry the mushrooms a bit," says Edgar.

"Crispy?"

"Borderline crispy."

"And the butter browned."

"Yes, browned butter."

"What would you like to drink, Anna?"

"Apple juice."

"And a glass for you?"

"I think I'll allow myself a glass of the one from the Loire . . . ,"
says Edgar.

"Savennières Clos?"

"Clos de la Coulée."

"Coulée it is, then."

BOAT

EVERY BIRD SINGS WITH ITS OWN BEAK, THE
Maître d' says. This applies not least to Raymond. He draws out
his vowels when he speaks. When he comes to order food, these
long vowels blend with the notes being produced by the fat fingers
of Old Johansen playing away up on the mezzanine. Old Johansen
has drifted into a Rachmaninoff lullaby; it's beautiful, but also
fairly slow and deeply tedious, I must say, a strange choice for this
time of day. The woozy Raymond orders entrecôte with the tune
tinkling away in the background. He has a deep voice, Raymond.
He sounds like a baritone. His order becomes some kind of miniature musical. He wants the entrecôte done medium well, and for
the sauceboat to be "compleeeeetely" full of béarnaise, he says. To
the brim. He adds that he only needs half a portion of onion compote. I say, "Wonderful."

On the whole, *mastering* speech, says Edgar, is primarily a case
of ignoring the embarrassing untruths we deliver in every sentence

construction. Untruths and inaccuracies, not least. Raymond doesn't struggle with that. His order of entrecôte and a full-to-the-brim sauceboat, which he delivers in harmony with the music, is a joy to the auricles. The ears. To us waiters, who might find ourselves dealing with all kinds of stuttering during orders, it's nice, from time to time, to be served a decent order, if I can put it like that.

Bratland is worse. His language doesn't add up; the syntax creaks and groans. The order goes wrong. "If you wait two minutes, I'll write up the day's specials on the board," I say. "Why can't you just say them?" Bratland asks. "I like to write," I say. I bring out the three-legged stool, climb up onto it, and stretch as far as I can: the board is high up; everyone needs to see it. As I reach the *d* in "tournedos," the chalk makes a shrieking sound which causes Bratland to swear. He digs one finger into his ear. I continue with "coq au vin," the chalk screeches, and Bratland swears again. "You're cutting my favorite music to shreds with your racket," he says. I ignore him and draw a firm line between the food and wine recommendations; the chalk squeals so loudly that Bratland huffs and puffs again. "Like a bradawl to the brain," he mumbles. I put away the stool and point to the board. Bratland squints. "I can't read that scrawl," he says. I explain that it says tournedos and coq au vin, but the truth is that I've written "turdonés" and "couq au vergin."

"I don't want that anyway," says Bratland.

"Wonderful," I say. Sellers orders confit duck thigh, like always.

"The *petits pois* are still ripening?" he asks rhetorically.

"They're far from full maturity."

"You know, I want them basically *unripe*."

"They're absolutely verging on unripe."

"And could you ask the chef to add a tiny splash of veal gravy to the thyme gravy?"

"Of course," I say.

•

The dinner guests start to arrive. Edgar and Anna's food is ready, and I take it out to them. Anna genuinely claps her hands as I place the lasagne on the table.

She is probably in the last six months of still making such adorable outbursts. They peter out and disappear for good after kids turn ten, don't they? Everything adorable gets phased out and replaced by something different. Some unenchanting trait. What is the opposite of "delightful"? "Despicable." "Adult." The chef's lasagne is fantastic, served to Anna in a small earthenware dish and still boiling and sizzling.

"It's red-hot," I say.

"I know that." Anna smiles.

"They're starting to get lively over there," says Edgar.

"Who?" Anna asks.

"Them around that table," says Edgar, nodding to Sellers's alcoholic milieu.

"What's wrong with them?" says Anna.

"They've drunk many beers," I say.

"How does that work for you?" says Edgar.

"How what?"

"Them carrying on like that?"

"It's who they are," I say.

"I'm just asking," says Edgar. He knows that Sellers is given a long leash in here.

"I have to move on."

"Indeed, they want their food now," Edgar says, making a grandiose gesture towards Sellers and the group.

I serve everything as ordered, with the exception of the sauce-boat for Raymond, which I not only do not fill to the brim, I put provocatively little béarnaise in. Raymond wrings his hands as I place it on his plate.

"Goodness me," he says with that singing, deep voice. Without a murmur, I take the sauceboat back to the kitchen and fill it all the way as he requested.

"Is this some kind of performance?" he asks when I come back.

"I beg your pardon?" I say.

"Are you making these serving mistakes on purpose?"

"Are you stealing our shenanigans?" Bratland butts in.

I move my head, neither a nod nor a shake. It's more an unwelcome jerk, a tic. It feels like I'm jolting awake after nodding off for a second. Bratland sneezes, which sounds like someone has slapped his face.

"You're a good waiter," says Raymond. "You know full well what I asked for. I asked for the sauceboat to be full to the brim.

Then you come out here with a scant boat. Next, you fill it to the brim and act like nothing has happened."

"Don't you start, too," Sellers says, either to Raymond or to me, I'm not sure.

"The boat is full now," I say as Raymond says: "It's not me stirring things up."

"Let it lie," says Sellers.

"Why take a walk with the cursed boat first?" says Raymond.

"Forget the boat," Sellers orders.

"It's dropped," Raymond says, holding up his hands in surrender.

Sellers steers a large chunk of duck thigh to his mouth. He chews discriminatingly. "Not much veal sauce in this," he says.

"I asked the chef to add a little."

"I think he forgot."

"He usually pays attention," I say.

"Then you'll have to drill him again," says Sellers.

"The chef is his own man."

"Ah, is he cooking for freedom in there?" says Sellers.

"The question isn't free *from* what but free *for* what," I say.

"Well, aren't we combative today," says Sellers.

I clap my hands together and walk through the restaurant, over to the bar, in a wide arc, where I collect a rancid, disappointing chardonnay, go back to table thirteen, and fill Bratland's glass to the brim without him asking for a top-up. He responds by taking a sip so large that his eyes snap back in his head.

CRITIQUE OF THE FEMALE BODY

THE CHILD LADY GETS UP FROM THE MARBLE-TOPPED table by the entrance and walks over to Sellers's avant-gardist alcohol table. The Bar Manager, the Maître d', and I all observe this. What business does she have with Sellers? She exchanges a few words with the intoxicated man and introduces herself with the same choreography she used on the Pig, Graham, and, to an extent, also on me. The Child Lady never creates anything new, I think; she just re-creates herself.

Eyebrows are further raised when she tips forward and grants Sellers what can only be described as a bear hug. All of her grace is released into his open arms. He wraps them around her and squeezes. Then he holds her in place, with an adult hand on the back of her head, in a prolonged, solid *knus*, as they say in Danish, the language of Europe's deceitful people.

The Bar Manager leans in and whispers that it's astounding

that she suits these men as well as she does the others. Spending time with both the Pig and Sellers on the same day is an artful move. It's to do with something deeper than grace, she says. When you look at this woman, you might suspect that there exists no beautiful surface without terrible depths behind it.

"But does she know them?"

"We'll see," says the Bar Manager. She's in a good place now.

The embrace ends, and the Child Lady's hands remain on Sellers's shoulders as they hold each other's gaze like old friends. They hug again. Then she giggles. She turns to the two other drunks in Sellers's group and sits down between them, on a chair which she most boldly pulls from table eleven. All I can do is set another place.

"Thank you, but I've just eaten," she says to me. Oh yes? Have the mushrooms I arranged been lost in oblivion? The order I fulfilled under an hour ago, has it been forgotten? Is she trying to cover up this double play, this overlapping, by feigning ignorance, suddenly sitting here at Sellers's table? With brisk movements, I undo my setting a place for her. I pick up the cutlery, napkin, and glass in reverse order, as though I'm being played backwards. It's impossible not to exhibit my bandaged hand, the punctured and covered blister. Maybe it's my imagination, but I feel like the Child Lady, Sellers, and not least the razor-sharp Raymond are watching it.

"I'll take a glass of pinot noir," the Child Lady says.

"*Jawohl*," I say firmly.

I spin around in confusion and run the crumber over a couple of departed tables. What am I saying? This is madness. She wants pinot noir now? What does that mean vis-à-vis the Pig's white burgundy? With age, it takes so little for something to go wrong in me. If I think of one thing or another, it goes wrong. If I see this person or that, it goes wrong. If I don't master this or the other, new wrong-going. The constant feeling that there—*there*—it went wrong. Oh no. It went wrong again. Why do things never work out for me? Not that anything ever actually goes wrong. But there is wrongness in me when the Child Lady sits down at Sellers's table. I blurt out German words which belong neither here nor there.

There's something about the Child Lady's age. She looks disproportionately young. At the same time, she seems so aged and experienced that she appears fatigued and slightly worn. How old is she? She's porno-old. She wears a number of rings on her fingers, indicating capital at its most serious. One of them sits on the knuckle of her middle finger, glittering and quivering like only diamonds can—it's almost baroque, I want to say—but she makes it go with the rest of her getup, which is a combination of expensive design and piece goods. I can see both Miu Miu and Dries van Noten, plus a slightly weak Balenciaga, and at the very bottom a surprising pair of shoes. They're relatively clumpy and colorful, with thick tongues like old skater shoes. But they are surely new; they could be new editions. Airwalks, maybe? What an idea. The Child Lady looks like a heavily made-up kid. When I arrive with the pinot noir and lean forwards with my acute stoop, I think that it might be age which makes her child's face seem more defined, sharper, that she's not so heavily made up after all. I let the wineglass approach the table without a sound and think that I mustn't turn towards her now; I'm not crazy; I can't turn around and stare her in the face. You don't stare your guests in the face from close-up. But I'm interested in this notion of makeup versus age. I'm reluctant to admit it, but standing here, with the glass still making its way towards the table, I get the urge to turn my head to the left and give the Child Lady's face a good stare. I arc over her right shoulder and let the glass silently meet the covered tabletop. I can feel her warmth, I'm so close. She gives off a faint scent of . . . the 1980s. Almost masculine. What is that smell? I hold the stem for a moment while I lean over her, in my handsome waiter's jacket, in my waiter's trousers, in my worn but still solid and well-cared-for shoes. My trusty shoes. That's how I'm standing, with my dry hair and my so-called nerve face, which I always try to tighten or hide behind my mustache. That's how I'm standing, thinking that it would be interesting to inspect the relationship between makeup and age on the Child Lady's face. So I turn and stare. She looks back. The distance between the tips of our noses—hers Greek, mine prominent—is the breadth of two Swedish sourdough loaves, no more. I should never have arranged this "meeting." She parts her lips and teeth, her mouth, in other words, pulls her tongue down from the palate with a click, and says: "*Jawohl.*"

I slowly loosen my grip on the elegant stem, filled with a light, good wine made from the Côte d'Ors's big grapes, pinot noir, and pull my hand away. I place it next to the bandaged claw behind my back and try to stand up straight. My lumbar protests. I straighten myself up like a cadet, with a quiet grunt and a stern face, until I end up in some kind of vertical position. There's nothing to be said to her "*Jawohl.*"

•

Nabokov had a funny approach to interviews, Edgar has told me: he insisted on writing down his answers first, and sending them to the journalist, who could then work out the questions. Here's the answer: you tell me. And the question? What the hell are you going to do with yourself after this blunder?

Of the opportunities for withdrawal I have here at The Hills, every one is time limited. I can go into the kitchen to seek refuge with the chef, but he's probably irritable and vibey as usual. I can yap a bit with the regulars—I'm allowed to spend more time on them than the others. I can go down to the cellar to fetch things, but that's something I tend to avoid, as I've already said. I often get a chaotic feeling down there. I've already done a loop with the crumber. I charge over to Edgar and Anna.

"Everything OK here?" I say formally.

"Yes," says Anna. She has eaten most of her lasagne.

"Slow going over there?" says Edgar.

"It is what it is," I say.

"Yes . . . and that latest addition complicated things, I suppose."

"What?"

"Well, do you know who she is?"

What is Edgar suggesting? Does he know her? I have a sinking feeling.

"Excuse me?"

"Her, the girl."

Her, the girl? Is he suddenly a specialist in the Child Lady? I stare at him but can't read his tight face. God forbid. The perfume. Was the perfume for her? It was musk she smelled of. What kind of charade is Edgar playing? Does he have an interest in the Child Lady? Is he speaking with a forked tongue? It's years since he announced his distance to the opposite sex. His distaste. But what's going on now? This might sound unfair and immature— he said that time—but the female body has lost its appeal. Here comes a critique of the female body, Edgar said. That was what he called it. A critique of the female body. I nodded and smiled, the way I always do. There are two reasons, he said. That was how he put it; logically. On the one hand, and this is nothing new: the mediated, maintained, tuned, harmonized, sculpted female body hasn't just made the ordinary, standard, common, everyday body that the vast majority of women possess superfluous. The mediated female body has made the day-to-day female body *unbearable*. The everyday body has no appeal because the mediated female body is constantly forced onto us. Fair enough. But on the other hand, the mediated and seemingly attractive female body—the one left as an object of desire now that the everyday body is over—is linked to the most vile form of monetary turnover, to such a degree that it voids itself as being attractive time and time again. It's a body which, if you stare at it, stares back. And it's the eyes of the hawker you're looking at. The tanned woman's body, with hundreds of thousands of squats on its résumé, and millions of followers on sharing platforms, is the hawker's face mask. He has pulled that woman's skin over his skull and is staring back at you like some kind of Leatherface, says Edgar. Anna had been there that time, too, but she was quite small, maybe in the first or second year of school. She had an exercise book with her. Edgar couldn't have said all this in front of her now. Do you know, girls, those of you aspiring to the mediated body, he said, how idiotic you look when you follow the nasty hawker's dictate? Do you see? He was pointing his finger then, literally. I can tell you the following: it makes you look retarded. The body you're striving for is ideological. It's the hawker's ideology camouflaged by skin. All I see is the sly hawker, said Edgar. And the hawker's plan doesn't make me lustful, let me tell you. Excuse me, but isn't it time these women covered themselves up a bit? This exposition of meat and flesh can't go on. Whenever the sun comes out, and we're going to the shop or out for a coffee, they force us to look at their hideous ass cheeks hanging out of their too-short denim shorts. Why do I have to have these sad cheeks in my field of vision, making me stare and see the hawker staring back at me? How retarded can they be? I see cleavage. Cover yourselves up, I'm saying. I see a navel. Cover it up. We don't want to see your navel. We never want to see thighs. The sight of a stupid, stupid female ass is the last thing we need to see now, in these times. It's sad for you. It's sad for us. It's like we're reading an ironic epilogue. The female body is a freed slave who has come back to tyrannize her former owner. Look here: everyone has strings up their butt cracks. The female body has become synonymous with the hawker's business interests. That's how Edgar talked. But now he has met the Child Lady and calls her "her, the girl"; he's changed his tune.

PART IV

SLEEP

EVERY MORNING I'M STUPID ENOUGH TO CHECK MY phone when I wake up. Today, still lying in bed, I had to relate to a video comparing the agile jumps of animals with those of athletes. An automated five-necked lute playing a tune on itself with some kind of robotic fingers. A teenager who made a functioning Luger out of straws. A clip of a drunk man (The Baltics? Russia?) who managed to stumble *into* a dump truck and disappear. Two unfaithful women being stoned in the Middle East. A Brazilian boy refusing to eat chicken wings because he's seen the film *Chicken Run*. A debate about the Californian drought and Nestlé. An article about Baudelaire's hash consumption. A swing bridge in India decorated with thousands of grotesque little cloth dolls. A sad Ford Mondeo advert. A Sami teenager's singing making a female foreign minister (Spanish? Polish?) cry. Because of this, I'm already wrecked by the time I get to The Hills to start the morning shift.

Old Johansen's liver-spotted hands dance across the piano keys on the mezzanine. I thought the Maître d' had forbidden him from playing it, but he is actually playing Pachelbel's Canon for three violins and basso continuo, his Canon in D Major. The piece doesn't sound patent on the grand piano. Old Johansen has, however, sharpened it a little, making it more difficult to recognize, which is possibly why he's getting away with it. Pachelbel's Canon for piano, however flabby it might be, is still preferable to a lot of other things. Rap music drones away out there.

I've attached the *Zeitungsspanner*s to the spines of the newspapers and started serving cappuccinos, espressos, americanos, and one freshly baked croissant after another. In between making espressos, the Bar Manager is adjusting an uncomfortable ring, as one calls it; she rubs her finger, the ringless one. Representatives of the adult world of conversation and commerce, as it's also known, come in one by one, ordering what they want to put in their mouths, which, as a rule, is something coffee-based, followed by baked goods. Who said that the concept of *living well* was a craze for times of crisis? Was it Balzac? Was it Cioran? If these aren't times of crisis, I don't know. Sometimes, when I overhear what is said at the tables, it's not really possible to distinguish between genuine statements and parody. I have real trouble telling sincerity from satire. The farce of everyday life seeps in here at The Hills as well, where we try to keep it at bay through rigid routines. You can probably assume that businessmen, functionaries, and lawyers don't parody their own world over their morning coffee, but it sure seems like it. Today I opened the bandage at the crack of dawn.

The blister looks horrendous. The skin is pale and dead and loose. I wrapped it back up with the same bandage.

The Bar Manager has tried to talk to me about how things unfolded yesterday evening and night three times now, but I wriggle out of it. I fetch the coffees she places on the counter and carry them over to their orderers. Are they called orderers? The people who order. The guests. The customers. The askers. The people who ask for something coffee-based, to be followed by baked goods. I won't let myself be fooled; I don't want to talk about yesterday. I've got enough to think about, I don't need to speculate about Sellers and the Child Lady, and, worse, Edgar and the Child Lady. I'm like a shuttle service with coffees in my hands. Cof-fees. Coffee cups. As long as the Bar Manager places a coffee or two cof-fees on the counter, she won't get any conversation about yesterday out of me.

She just stood there glaring all evening anyway, passively, while I ran around serving, like a headless chicken, and, not least, made sure Anna was OK while Edgar went over to Sellers's table and strutted his stuff with handshakes and laughter. What crazy rashness he was up to, Edgar. You don't go over to other people's tables like that, like some autograph hunter; you just don't. He was even asked to sit down, between the Child Lady and Sellers. I had to serve him while he sat there on his throne. He let me carry over one Moretti after the other. It behooved me to serve. Behooved? Anna had immersed herself in her book over at the other table, drinking cocoa for what seemed to me—and probably also to her—like an eternity.

Edgar had given her a fantasy book—not exactly ambitious, in other words. I tried asking Anna about the plot but didn't really get what it was about. A group of teenagers were being kept as "tear slaves" in a dystopian, futuristic dictatorship. Thanks to a serious shortage of H_2O, human tears were a resource, and certain poor, un-free creatures (teens) were forced to cry in a factory. No, that can't be right. That seems too thin, even for fantasy. Even for fantasy? What do I know about fantasy? Doesn't Anna have school tomorrow? I eventually had to ask Edgar. It was almost a quarter to eleven. Edgar, cackling, smiling, between the Child Lady and Sellers. He took the floor every now and again, I could see. He went on about both this and that, and had the entire table listening. The clock struck ten past eleven before he pulled himself together and left, dragging an overtired Anna with him. Indefensibly late for a school child, you could say. I left shortly after. Sellers, the Child Lady, Bratland, and Raymond continued their bacchanal—yes, that's the word the Bar Manager chooses to use; their bacchanal continued until the restaurant closed, well into the night. The Child Lady was there until the very end, says the Bar Manager, tête-à-tête with Sellers. They were talking about cars, she says. That can't be right, I say. Yes, they were completely absorbed in a conversation about automobiles, the car industry, different models. It looked like autism for two, she claims. The old 250 Lusso is a masterpiece, Sellers had said. Can you call "Pinin" Farina anything but a master? the Child Lady had replied. All this while I slept.

And what do you know? Here comes the Child Lady, so early: here she comes through the curtain, pushing it to one side. It's only a quarter past seven. It is she? I'm not sure. It's like her. Yes, it is she. Isn't it? She looks like herself. She looks like a thousand others. But it is she, it has to be. There's nothing special about the Child Lady, and in a way that's her beauty. Fresh as the morning dew, wrinkle-free, featureless, pretty. She looks rested. She sits down at the bar, right in front of the Bar Manager, who will be making a firm mental note of that, if I know her right. What's her order? Quadruple espresso. Another quadruple espresso. Doesn't she sleep? As Edgar often says, sleep is good. Sleep is an uncompromising break from the thieving of time that the hawker subjects us to. Edgar likes to sleep. The majority of seemingly irreducible necessities in life—hunger, thirst, friendship, desire— have been rediscovered in financial forms, so to speak. Sleep is a human need and a "dead' interval which can't immediately be colonized or placed under the hawker's yoke, Edgar often says, slightly clumsily, with his index finger pointing again. In that sense, sleep remains an anomaly, an unknown territory for the hawker. Despite all the research in the field, sleep continues to frustrate and make strategies for exploiting or reshaping it to the hawker's wishes impossible, Edgar says. It's not bed manufacturers I'm talking about here. Not the psychoanalysts, either, with their dream reading. The fascinating truth is that nothing of value can, as yet, be extracted from sleep itself.

But doesn't the Child Lady sleep? She just keeps coming back

like an itch or a flu or the tax man. I'm all for predictability and rep-
etition, but the routine of being exposed to the Child Lady every
day . . . I'm not so sure. Her steady coming makes everything else
wobbly. She's wearing crisp, fresh clothes. No kinks in her hair.
Absolutely no bags beneath her eyes. She looks productive. She sits
there, sipping her quadruple espresso, just a short time after partic-
ipating in the bacchanal around Sellers's table. Yes, I'm calling it a
bacchanal, too, even if it wasn't, strictly speaking, a "sumptuous celebration of the grape." Sellers's bacchanal is more a celebration of *the
flaky*, it might seem. A celebration of ongoing, persistent procras-
tination, time wasting, with tormenting idleness the consequence.
Flake. An indulgence of inactivity and inept behavior. How can the
Child Lady be so energetic after taking part in that all night?

She reaches for an object. Sometimes, for brief moments, it's
as though my language becomes confused. One word or another
might dissolve completely, and I can't come up with it when I need
it. Right now, I can't think of the word for the object lying on the
counter. It's panicky. As I lose the ability to attach words to things,
like now with this object of the Child Lady's, I become one great big
eye, an enormous retina. What's it called? Aphasia? Can you develop
aphasia without a stroke, without a tumor on the brain or some
other damage? The object is colorful. She grasps it and retrieves
something, picks up or produces something; she pulls something
out, fishes something up, a telephone, which she then swipes across,
swipes up a number, and raises it to her lovely ear, which is decorated with a large, glittering earring—it must be a diamond.

THIRTEEN
MISSED CALLS

"I'M AT THE HILLS," I HEAR HER SAY. "NO, NO . . . YES,
I'm here now . . ."

She clears her throat and sounds like a small engine.

"For sure! I'm not kidding."

With that, she giggles quietly and turns away, as though she
wants to hide her laughter from the Bar Manager, and possibly also
from me, standing here like a statue. The Bar Manager has placed a
glass of water next to the Child Lady's coffee; it remains untouched.
The espresso goes down. Now she rubs her phone as she sips her
quadruple. She rubs and rubs the glass with her index and middle
fingers and stares at the screen. She leans forward, bends over it,
buffering the screen, you could say. I collect a plate and a cup from
the now-empty table three, where a Wiersholm, Mellbye & Bech
lawyer was just eating. As I set the cup and saucer on the bar, I cast
a long glance, as it's known, at the Child Lady's screen, but can see

precious little. Is she on social media? Probably. Now she's socializing, in a sense, through media which are social. Or? It's difficult if not impossible for me to say who she is socializing with and how. As long as I can't see the screen properly, I don't know a thing about who she interacts with, even if she is sitting right in front of me. And not just that. I honestly can't know whether she's reading or looking at pictures, either. I don't know if she's political, an activist, if she pays her bills, if she works, has sex, watches films, talks to her parents, goes to school, is buying clothes or furniture, maybe a car. It's impossible to know. Even if she is sitting there, in full view, as they say. Her hunching over the screen is and will be the same, regardless. The square centimeters of the screen have, in a sense, taken on a similar function to banknotes—the absolute translator of all things, I've thought, via Edgar. Work, leisure, pictures, relationships, knowledge, nonsense, text, bullying and drudgery, buying and exchanging, production and unrestrained consumption, birds and fish, endless inventiveness and wild control, desire and systems—everything can be translated into money, and all this can be translated again to play out on the screen.

The majority of "things" become styled and trimmed down to fit the screen, just like all "things" are styled and reworked so that they can be turned into bills in one way or another. Banknotes and the screen are related. The screen is the banknote's window. The screen is the hawker's window. That's probably it. The hawker stares back up at you from the screen. He probably does. Especially at Edgar. The Child Lady raises her head before I manage to compose myself; I'm rubbing my hands on a kitchen towel embroidered with the restaurant logo, bleary-eyed, I can imagine, staring at a fixed point, as they say, insidious, demanding, worrying, staring at her, the Child Lady, for no good reason. She stares back. For a moment I see the hawker staring at me, the way he stares out from the screen. Now I see the Child Lady. Now the hawker's awful face is visible again. And now I see the Child Lady's immaculate face once more, and all I can do is fold the towel into a long rectangle which I lift up and bring down against the bar like a short bullwhip or baton. It makes a nice crack, and it looks like some kind of habit, hopefully, a ritual, a waiter's practice, something "French," something to symbolize a period, a full stop, the transition from one duty to another: I spin around and immediately start going over the tables with the incessant crumber; I *slash* away crumbs, croissant flakes, imagining that my sweeping looks experienced, but also feeling enormously bent and idiotic. The Child Lady jumped a little when I whipped the embroidered towel against the bar. She looked at me. Imagine the number of waiters and coachmen (now taxi drivers) who have quietly been forgotten by history. Imagine the number of men who have vanished into waiting work or driving, in Europe, over the years. The eternal coachman. The eternal waiter. There has been plenty of driving. There has been plenty of dishing out food and quenching thirst.

The Child Lady gives me a wave, and I go over. There's a distinct smell around her; I still believe it's musk. Unfortunately, I slept on one cheek last night, meaning I have a vertical crease from my eye down to the corner of my mouth. I must have been in the same position all night, because the crease won't go away. It makes me look considerably older than I am.

"Excuse me," she says.

I lean forward to suggest "attention"—yes, I'm actually leaning against the counter, and my hand is resting right next to her clutch. "Clutch" was the word I was looking for, that object of hers.

"Do you know what Sellers said to me yesterday?"

"Sellers?"

"Yes, Sellers."

"No."

"He said that I'm an obsessive thought."

"What?" I say.

The Child Lady giggles; she raises her hand to her mouth. I am—as I often am—left in the same position, unmoving, like poultry, fowl, because I don't understand. A new giggle forces its way out. It looks like she's trying to make a poor attempt to hide the fact that she is giggling from me. I'm standing there with my right hand on the counter and the bandaged blister behind my back. Even when she giggles, the Child Lady is at work, I think.

"Don't touch the clutch," she says.

I realize my hand is resting too close to the so-called clutch of hers, and I pull it back as though from a baking tray.

"And do you know what Edgar said to me?" she asks.

"Edgar?"

"Yes, you know. Edgar, your friend."

"Yes, I . . . ," I say.

"Do you know what he said?"

They're on first-name terms. It's one thing that she's in circulation, that she moves from the Pig's table to Sellers's, but that Edgar is now part of this circulation, this "scene," is disturbing. Yes, there I said it. Disturbing. How long has this been going on? Edgar played up for Sellers's table, that was easy to see. He turned it on for the Child Lady. Stood up straight. Gesticulated, moved a lot, virile. Everyone who comes into contact with the Child Lady becomes some kind of child lady themselves, it seems.

"Don't you want to hear?"

"Just a moment," I say, moving backwards like a crayfish. I have to get away.

The chef is busy chopping in the kitchen. What's being chopped? Isn't the early morning for poaching eggs? His chopping is firm; it feels like he's whacking my cranium. There's an old butcher's block behind him; I stand to one side of it. The block is at least fifty centimeters thick and equipped with an iron belt around the middle. The ceiling above the block—or the chopper, as the chef calls it—is just as black as the vaults above his gas hob; it's like a black abyss. There's an old-fashioned garlic press on top of the block, gray and well used, the plunger section itself almost black. Where does the Child Lady know Edgar from? I don't understand. There's a carton of twenty or thirty cherry tomatoes, and I push them into the garlic press one by one, squeezing and making some kind of tomato mush, ketchup, from the tomatoes, which runs straight onto the floor. What is the musk around the Child Lady? Is it Edgar's musk? Does he carry it around with him? Doesn't "musk" mean "testicle" in Sanskrit? What is Edgar up to? Has he given her *musk*?

"What are you doing?" says the chef.

"Me?" I say.

"Why are you making a mess? What have you done to my tomatoes?"

"I'll clean it up."

I move my head uncoordinatedly from right to left in search of a cloth.

"And you need to answer your phone," says the chef.

"What?"

"Your phone. It's been ringing nonstop in your locker."

My phone never rings "nonstop." As a rule, there are zero missed calls at the end of a working day. I never check my phone at work. There's nothing in my life worth ringing "nonstop" for. Repeated calls this early in the morning can only mean that something has gone wrong.

"I don't check my phone when I'm working," I say.

"Do I have to listen to it all day? I need the tomatoes."

"Not at all," I say. "Is it OK with you if I check it?"

"That's what I'm asking you to do."

"It's unauthorized to have phones. We'll have to tell the Maître d' it's an emergency."

"An emergency?"

"It probably is."

"Just check your phone."

"I'll get the tomatoes."

I go into the wardrobe corner and pull the ungodly device from the pocket of my all-weather jacket. Edgar has called thirteen times. That's a bit much. Did something else happen yesterday? Was he too drunk when he left with Anna? Is someone hurt? Why am I asking myself? Wouldn't it be better to ring him? Can I allow myself to call back?

"Can I allow myself to call back?" I ask the chef.

"Allow yourself."

Edgar answers; he *takes it* in a second, with a huff and a clearing of the throat, and explains that he has to travel to Copenhagen on "urgent business" and wonders whether Anna can come down to The Hills after school. The trip is work related, he says. She can just sit there. What? I say. She's used to it, says Edgar. You don't have to keep her entertained. No, no, I answer. Just give her a bit of food, says Edgar. I see myself as highly conflict averse, but if I don't want my nerves to be the end of me, I need to toughen up and explain that it's stressful for me to be responsible for Anna while I'm working. Edgar has no sympathy for that. Your job's pure routine, he says. Isn't that the whole point? Put food in front of the girl and chat for ten minutes, and the job's done. Give her a Cola. She doesn't need special treatment. She'll do her homework and read. It's easy, he says. We're talking about a child. One child is nothing; two are like ten, so they say, says Edgar. She just needs the food on credit, that's the only difference. Food *on credit*? He won't be back late, he says. I'll pick her up in good time, he says. In good time like yesterday? I ask with a bitter undertone. Hey, watch it. Edgar becomes sharp. How bad was it yesterday? Isn't he allowed to let loose once in a while? Isn't he a single parent, and doesn't he stay at home, night after night, practically alone, in his flat, year in and year out? Hasn't his mother died? Does he have anyone else to help? Is Anna's mother a pill-popping wreck or not? Aren't I a friend? Is it so much to ask? All this is asked. No, of course it's not, I reply. It's not too much to ask. When you put it like that. You can send Anna over after school. Why this kind of onslaught? He is attacking me with his child.

ROMANESCO

THE CHEF'S BACK IS HUNCHED AND ROUNDED.

"I need tomatoes. You have to fetch tomatoes," he says.

"What?"

"Four minutes."

"Where are they?"

"The cellar."

I'm standing by the cellar hatch, feeling my nerve endings twitching and taking in the fact that Sigurd the Crusader tramped around these square meters 885 years ago. This is where he walked, mistress's son Sigurd, barely forty years old. He had already been king for twenty-six years, taciturn, not kind, but good to his friends, and faithful. And here I am, in the same place, ready to open the cellar hatch and go down to fetch trusses of tomatoes, worrying in an abstract sense. Yes, the distance between what happened when Sigurd walked here and what is happening right now has to be seen as infinite. An infinite distance, seen from a human point of view, but a distance equal to zero from a geographic perspective. He stood *here*, Sigurd, in Oslo, about to die after an utterly epic life. A phenomenal life. After having sabered down Muslims on the edge of Europe. "Sabered" might be the wrong word in this context: he stabbed them with swords, at least, possibly a bearded axe. I've never stabbed a Muslim. I can't find the right key for the padlock; it's difficult to hold the heavy chain in my bandaged hand while I fiddle with the chef's enormous bunch of keys. Why is it so huge? The padlock and chain are bitingly cold, and my hand goes numb. My breathing is shallowing. I produce brief bursts of frost smoke. The hatch is as heavy as lead; the stairs are steep and perilous, with steps worn down by use. But why is the light on? The bulb hanging in the first corridor is burning brightly. I'm stooping at the bottom of the stairs. The back of my head is touching the ceiling, it's so low. And I thought The Hills had high ceilings. I glare diagonally downwards, towards where the fork in the passage is supposed to be. Is there someone down here?

"Hello?"

The countless drawers, cabinets, and shutters disappear in the obscurity of the central corridor before the much-discussed fork appears. The tomatoes are kept to the left, I know, along with the other fruit, in the drawer section beside what looks like a dashboard. Tomatoes are classed as vegetables in many Norwegian homes, but botanically speaking they're fruits, with large, juicy, and not least nutritious seeds. Using my right hand, I fumble down to the fork in the corridor; I press the blistered hand against my thigh. Below, at knee height, beneath a "fore-drawer," you're supposed to be able to turn on the light in the next section, according to the chef. It's not easy. What is a fore-drawer? My fingers run beneath a series of five drawers with sloping fronts. Could these be fore-drawers? All I can feel is soil or soot, something dry, powdery. Beyond these, I reach behind something resembling a bureau. I'm down on my knees and an elbow, thanks to my injured hand. I pull on a small knob and the light comes on. I look at the panel above me. Dashboard? Are these fuses? It can't be climate control? The wall where the tomatoes and other fruit are kept is divided into a number of new drawer sections. A truss or two are sticking out.

"Yes, hello," I hear behind me; I'm still on all fours.

Jittery and bent-backed, I manage to crawl into a half-standing position and stare straight at the Maître d'. What's he doing down here?

"What are you doing down here?"

"What am I doing down here?"

The Maître d' has no expression; all he really does is hold his big face in front of mine.

"How's it going?"

"How is it going? What do you mean?" he says.

"No . . . of course."

"We need the small pewter plates for the sticks of butter."

"Aha," I say, forming a small OK sign with my thumb and index finger.

The pewter plates he's talking about are the sweetest little things. They're Danish, and they have a banner engraved around the edge, as well as the previous owner's initials, dated 1789, actually. There's an encircled anchor and a gull stamped on the back. They've been in the Hill family's possession, incredibly, since three-quarters of a century before the restaurant opened. The Danish pewter plates have a diameter of eight centimeters. It would be an exaggeration to say that the bags beneath the Maître d's eyes were as big as pewter plates, but they are big, those bags, so it doesn't seem an unreasonable comparison.

"Well . . . hunger knows no friend but its feeder," he says with a clearing of the throat, which sends the unmistakable scent of Kremlyovskaya up my nose. Then he turns, after another brief stare, and crawls up the awfully steep stairs.

"You'll have to get up."

The idea that vodka doesn't betray secret drinking is only half-true, I think to myself.

The vegetables are on the opposite wall, some of them in open drawers, and between the cauliflower and broccoli, beneath an overgrown and fairly ugly turnip and some turnip rape—which is hardier than rape, so they say—are three impressive Romanescos. I like Romanesco. Romanesque cauliflower is something I've always liked. Not the taste, but the appearance. Not that it's all that original, but I've always been fascinated by the Romanesco's fractal shape. It's almost too much. It's not necessarily tasteful, visually, the Romanesco. But you can't cast judgment on its tastiness if it's naturally spectacular, can you? I feel a deep, childish joy whenever I see a Romanesco. Has Anna seen a Romanesco? Probably not. I decide to take one up so she can see it later. If she's bored. After her homework is done and the fantasy has been read, when the conversation with me dries up. I will keep her busy. I will keep her entertained. I will dig a moat around her with my routines.

THE FLORIST

IT'S EIGHT IN THE MORNING, I'M EXHAUSTED ALREADY, and it's Friday, which means the florist is blooming by the back door, to put it glibly. The florist does his floristry a couple of times a week, and always on Fridays, so that the flower arrangements are fresh and crisp for the weekend. I've got my arms full of tomatoes and the Romanesco, and I ask him to go in. The florist is the least florist-like man you can imagine: he's no gossipmonger, and he's not of unconventional preferences. He doesn't have glasses, the hairdo, scarves, or challengingly cut clothes. He's young and looks more like a craftsman from the Balkans than a florist. But he takes his floristry all the more seriously for it, and offers both flower arrangement and design. He even grows some of the flowers himself, I know, and sells these flowers, which means that much of the floristry is covered by his business. He leaves the floristics itself, however, alone. I asked him about it once and was given a brief, dismissive answer. I know he has a fundamentally ikebana philosophy adapted to a traditional, European customer base. Sure enough, he stays away from contemporary European arrangements, with their focus on asymmetry, negative space, dramatic pauses, and silly counterpoints. I nod tensely at the door stopper to hint that he should use it while he's bringing the bunches of flowers in and out of the algae-green Berlingo parked in The Hills's own parking space. As though he doesn't know that already, about the door stopper. As though he hasn't been here before. As though he doesn't bring flowers to The Hills twice a week. My lack of tact complicates situations.

"Did I ask for Romanesco?" asks the chef.

"Not at all," I say.

"Then what's this?"

"Romanesco."

The chef gives me a dead look.

"I brought it up to show Anna. I thought it might be fun."

"Anna . . ."

"Yeah, she's coming here after school. She has to stay for a while."

"Ah."

"Edgar, her father, is in Copenhagen on business."

". . ."

"So she has to stay here a while."

". . ."

"I thought the Romanesco could be something."

If I have the ability to make conversations drag, the chef is the grand master of driving them into the ditch. We stand there for a second, staring at one another and breathing, him through his flat nose, me through my mustachioed mouth. He places the tomatoes on a chopping board and turns his back to me. I go back out into the restaurant. The twitching in my head is out of time with the steps my legs are taking, like a fowl again, something from the Galliformes order. And as I lock eyes with the Child Lady, I feel the damn Romanesco weighing heavily in my right hand. Why haven't I put it down? Why have I brought a cauliflower out into the restaurant? The Child Lady looks at the vegetable and then up at me. She waves and I, still birdlike in my movements, can't see any other possibility than to skip/waddle/strut over with the cauliflower in one hand and the blister/flap in the other. She places her phone on the counter, screen up. I wish I had another face to give you, another visage to present. I would have liked to give you the face I had, say, twelve to fourteen years ago. But that face is gone. It doesn't exist anymore. Like so many other things. The only face I have is this one. A mug exposed to considerable wear and tear. I can feel it, the damage, the age, when she, decay-free, ageless, stares at it, my face.

"That's some vegetable," she says.

"Yes . . ."

"Is it a . . . ?"

"A kind of cauliflower."

"Yes." She smiles.

"Romanesco, it's called. You can taste that it's related to broccoli."

"Oh really?"

"Yes."

". . ."

"And look at this," I say, lifting the vegetable to her face.

"My word."

"Yeah, maybe you can see that it's intricate."

"Yes, wow."

"You could imagine Benoit Mandelbrot having drawn it," I say, followed by a "Heh," which is a bit too loud; it sounds like a cough, a clearing of the throat; the sound comes from the roof of my mouth.

". . ."

"I like this kind of complex or impossible visuality," I continue, now out of control.

"Such bottomless visualities."

I'm holding the Romanesco with straight fingers, like a small skull, studying it with narrow eyes before I hear myself blurt out the following train of thought:

"Think how nice it was in Old Europe, not even that far back in time, when, for example, you might step through a door and up a staircase and find M. C. Escher cutting his impossible geometric figures onto wood blocks with the greatest of accuracy. So pleasant. He carved absurd and impossible perspectives into his wooden blocks, with the focus of a scientist, and then he made those into beautiful woodcuts. That was that. Enjoyable for him to make. Beautiful for us to look at. Things aren't like that anymore.

It's no longer possible for us to go to the market in Nuremberg and see Albrecht Dürer and his wife, Agnes, née Frey, in the stall she set up next to the fruit and vegetable sellers to sell her husband's prints. The childless Dürer couple went to fair-like events in Leipzig and Frankfurt and offered divinely inspired prints to the everyman for good money. No epic genius sells prints on that square anymore. You can forget it. Now it's all *döner* kebabs and broken-phone-screen repairmen everywhere. Poor Europe. You can get your phone fixed, that much is certain."

The Child Lady is listening. Is she taking it in? I'm floundering. It's healthy, I say now. Antioxidants are important, I say. And isn't that the hallmark of the moron? People who talk about things they have no idea about always talk about antioxidants. Antioxidants protect against the body's production of free radicals, I say. They're important for preventing cancer, among other things. Too many free radicals can damage our cells. You find antioxidants in rose hips and walnuts. In sour cherries and sunflower seeds. Blueberries. And tea. And chocolate! Did you know that? No, the Child Lady didn't. Maybe you know what I'm getting at here? No, she's not sure. Well, vegetables are also full of antioxidants. Red cabbage and kale. And maybe broccoli in particular. And who's broccoli's neighbor? The Child Lady points to the cabbage. Exactly! The Romanesco.

This is a full-on crisis. I'm left standing with the vegetable in my hand, and my lips shaped like the mouth of a bottle for a few seconds before. In panic, I shout at the florist, who has just come out of the kitchen with a huge bouquet of lilies in his arms.

"Hey!"

The florist stops. I place the cabbage on the counter.

"Can you cut off the stamen so the lilies don't start smelling like manure in two days?"

"Of course . . ."

"Good. Don't put it off, please."

"OK."

"And you have to *pinch* them off with your fingers, ideally with paper in between. They stain horribly."

"I know that," the florist says with a puzzled face.

I've set the level of my voice too high, but I can't give in now, and drag it out a little more.

"Good."

"Could I have the bill?" says the Child Lady. Her smoothness makes her difficult to read. If she's disappointed, offended, if she's trying to get away in panic, or if she just wants the bill, it's impossible to say. Her face is like an unplugged flat screen, a so-called smart TV without power. She allows her peepholes to cling to me, with their almost bluish whites, until I force out a matter-of-fact, reserved, concise, professional, firm, desperate "Of course" and top that "Of course" off with a nod so severe that a lock of hair falls forward onto my forehead. I must look like a clown. With one hand outstretched, resembling a *Heil Hitler* more than anything else, I shout to the Bar Manager that there's a request to pay at this end of the bar. "There's a request to pay" are the actual words I use. The Bar Manager places the bill on a little plate, which I carry from the till over to the Child Lady. The plate is from Rörstrand, I know that.

"The bill for a quadruple espresso presented on a small faience plate," I say, letting the plate land gently, like a little bird, in front of her.

"A what plate?" the Child Lady says.

"Faience."

"Which is?"

"*Fayance.*"

". . ."

"It's earthenware. Originally from Faenza. The factories in Delft tried to copy Chinese porcelain—white with blue detailing, you know. Faience became very popular."

"Ceramics?"

"Yes, you could say. They've been making faience at Rörstrand since the 1700s. Here in Norway, Egersund Fayancefabrik have been at it for over one hundred years. We've got a lot of Egersund in the cellar."

"I'm learning a lot today."

"But the majority of items from Egersund aren't faience."

"No?"

"They're stoneware."

"OK."

"They're in the cellar."

"In the cellar?"

"We've got a complex and deep cellar, right beneath here."

The Child Lady pulls an impressive wad of cash from her clutch while she studies the bill, which is resting with a discreet crease on the faience plate. There's nothing proportionate about the wad of cash and the price of the quadruple espresso. But the Child Lady still has to get them—the cash and the espresso—to communicate somehow.

"You're not interested in hearing what Edgar said yesterday, then," she says without looking at me.

What should I say to that? She uses her breath and the movement of her tongue to hoot out his name—"Edgar"—again.

"Edgar has never actually been in the cellar beneath here, under The Hills," I say. I pick up the Romanesco and weigh it in my hand; I let it bounce up and down.

"Never," I repeat.

"No?"

"No. Never." I place the cauliflower on the counter and turn it over so that the very tip of it is pointing at the Child Lady.

"But would he . . ."

"You know that the Norwegian word for waiter comes from the German *Kellner*, which really means 'cellar master'—derived from the Latin *cellarius*."

"No, that's news to me."

"Well, then."

The Child Lady looks up and gives me another smile. If you really want to talk about dental arches, the prime specimen is right here, in the Child Lady's mouth. Everything has to be straightened nowadays, I often think, but you can clearly see that correction and straightening have something going for them here, given that this dental arch has been straightened, something I'm assuming it has, unless it's natural after all, which is no less spectacular.

"That means you're the cellar master, then."

"I mean, in principle, no. I'm upstairs, well, but . . ."

"Since you're a *Kellner* and everything."

"No. I mean, it's an old term."

" 'Cellar door,' " she says, placing far too large a banknote on the plate.

"What?"

"The most beautiful words in the English language, wasn't that it? *'Slide down my cellar door . . .'* "

". . ."

"You know, the song."

"I'll just get your change," I say. "Excellent."

To my horror, she doesn't leave this time, either, but sits down at the marble-topped table over by the curtain. What is she? A moray eel lying rigidly in wait by the entrance of the hole?

OLD JOHANSEN

WE SEE THAT TOO LITTLE SLEEP IS UNHEALTHY FOR schoolwork. We see a clear relationship between a lack of sleep and underperformance. We see that. They said so on the radio this morning. They see such things, the people looking for them. We'll also see it in Anna later. When was she coming again? Four? Five? She didn't get much sleep last night, thanks to Edgar's eagerness to press himself onto Sellers and the group. We'll see a tired, slightly worn-out Anna when she comes in with her oversized schoolbag on those slim, bony shoulders, six to eight hours from now. How can they send her off with so many books?

She must have to walk with her back bent almost 45 degrees just so that she doesn't tip over and end up like an upside-down tortoise or beetle. Poor child. Poor innocent Anna.

Old Johansen is playing tunes, and they're sad, I want to say melancholy; are they expressing *the wretch*? The poor beggar? The bloke with the beggar's stick? Is Old Johansen on the mezzanine a wretch? He probably is. He began with Pachelbel this morning, and it's gone downhill since. It's rare for the Maître d' to allow Johansen to drape such a mourning cloak of music over the restaurant. We can't let him build up (down) to Anna's entrance like this.

What follows is something I've never done before in my time here at The Hills: I decide to twist my body up the spiral wrought-iron staircase, onto the mezzanine, up to Old Johansen. The staircase is an effort to climb. How does Old Johansen even manage it? He's as round as a barrel. I've never thought about it before, but he's always up there already when I get to work. I've never seen him climbing the stairs. Have I seen him go down? No. He's there when I leave, too. I *twist* up the stairs. From the top step, where I have to stand with my neck completely bent because of the low ceiling, I can see his shirt-clad back, divided by his antiquated braces with leather loops and buttonholes into a large, black X. (He probably chose these X-shaped suspenders over the Y-shaped ones because of his width; a hefty man like Old Johansen needs two anchoring points on the back of his trousers.)

"Johansen, what shift are you even working?"

Old Johansen lifts his chin up and slightly to the side; he doesn't jump at all, as though there are constantly people coming up onto the mezzanine, behind his back, asking unexpected questions.

"Pardon?"

"What shift are you working, Johansen?"

"The same shift I've always worked."

He's sitting on a double piano stool, a high-quality so-called duet stool, with two separate and adjustable seats, again because of his width, I'm assuming. The stool has a dial on each side, one for each seat, and the cushions are covered in first-class velvet in deep burgundy, almost oxblood. The actual body of the stool is made from heavily varnished beech. And this comes as something of a surprise: beneath the heels of Johansen's polished shoes is a pedal extender, an old-fashioned pedal footrest. So he's shorter than I thought, in relation to his width. Old Johansen is practically round.

"Hey, Johansen . . . ," I say.

"You're welcome," says Johansen.

("You're welcome"? Have I received something? What have I been given?)

"You know that the Maître d' thinks Pachelbel's Canon is a tad too melancholic? Since you started the morning with it, you've entered territory that's even more gloomy. Could you lighten it up a bit?"

"Pachelbel's Canon is in D major."

"OK, but can you just make it a bit less melancholic?"

"It is what it is. I can't make it any less melancholic. I don't know what you mean," Johansen says while he continues to produce smooth melancholy with all ten fingers.

"We've been asked whether you would be so kind as to lighten the mood a little."

Is Johansen a part of the mezzanine? One thing is the relationship between body width/spiral staircase. Another is the piles of notebooks and papers surrounding the piano. All kinds of printed matter and musical literature, it looks like, are stacked up against the walls. The arching of the vault begins no more than a meter and a half above the mezzanine floor, but this meter and a half is more or less covered in these piles. And, wouldn't you know it, the stickers on the wainscoting down in the restaurant have also made their way up here. They've crept up the spiral staircase: you can see them behind Johansen's stacks. Old, cracked cuttings, labels, and overlappings; in some places they're so yellowed and stained that it looks like they might have been coated with layers of coffee-colored shellac. At waist height, to the left, someone has drawn a series of musical notes on the wall; it looks like some kind of inexperienced scrawl: note heads, stems, and flags are clumsily drawn in charcoal or dry crayon, possibly chalk. In front of the notes, there are several stacks of plates, all different heights. I can see flat dining plates for solid food, deep soup bowls for liquid meals, and several serving plates, in addition to one stack after another of side plates. A number of them are the Egersund faience that I went on about to the Child Lady. Isn't the Maître d' constantly looking for these? There are piles of knives, forks, and spoons on the top plate of each stack, all soiled with food; it looks like Johansen has been stacking and collecting for a long time. The floor is covered in everything from bouquet glasses to fine crystal champagne flutes, all over the place; many of them have forks and other basic pieces of cutlery sticking up out of them. I can see a crab spoon peeping up from a finger bowl, also crystal, along with a set of snail tongs, four three-pronged fish forks, and, believe it or not, the finest caviar spade we have. Not far from Johansen's pedals, there is a pair of grape shears on top of a deer pan, plus a handful of gourmet spoons and the handsome game service inherited from Benjamin Hill himself. Who carries all this up here but not back down? What kind of gluttony is this?

"You've got an entire restaurant up here, Johansen," I say.

Johansen doesn't reply; instead he throws back his head slightly, making his hair shake. His hair is dry, like wire wool. There's a bit of length at the back of his neck, but on top it's completely thinned out, and he has halfheartedly pushed the hair at the side over his crown—it looks like some kind of Deleuzian comb-over frizz. When he shakes his head in a dramatic punctuation of one moment of the music or another, his hair sways firmly; it isn't "thrown"—a dry, hard swing, the way you can imagine tree moss swaying if the rock or trunk it's growing on is given a kick.

Almost imperceptibly, the notes coming from the piano become lighter and, as far as I can tell, less melancholy. Is Johansen obeying? Is he going for a major key? Or is this a modulation already in the piece? Old Johansen conjures the notes from the instrument with such ease. How is it possible for such fat, emperor-like fingers to move so freely over the keys? How heavy is the piano? What a monster. What a beast. My chest tightens at the thought of the instrument once having been hauled up here onto the mezzanine. It can't have come up the spiral stairs—that much is clear. But how? There's a hatch window beneath the vault to the right, but it's no more than sixty centimeters wide, so it can't have been that way, either. Did they cut through the roof at some point, to haul this monstrous musical instrument inside? Did they haul Old Johansen in at the same time?

"Is that Heifetz on the wall over there?" I ask, pointing—even though Johansen is sitting with his back to it—to a small, framed woodcut squeezed in and half-hidden behind the stacks.

"It's Heifetz," says Johansen.

"Funny, you can recognize him by the sharp nostrils."

"It's not much to look at. The cut was done by a forgotten Norwegian printmaker. No Heifetz, exactly," says Johansen.

"No, no Heifetz."

"Wonderful," says Johansen, still without turning around. The music is definitely lighter now. More lively.

"Great," I say, ready to go back downstairs.

"Can I stop You for a moment?"

He actually uses the formal address on me. I turn back and remember that I've been addressing Johansen informally for as long as I've been up here.

"Yeah?"

"I think You seem a bit frazzled."

"What?"

"I think You seem hectic."

"I'm not sure I understand."

"Shaky. Frail."

"Is that so?"

"It's like Winnicott claims," Johansen says, accompanied by his own now-lively playing: "The ego organizes defenses against breakdown of the ego-organization."

"And that is?"

"When the ego's organization falters, collapse rears its head, you know."

So I radiate wretchedness, even through my imaginary armor and shield of service, routine, and predictability. Old Johansen doesn't even need to turn around to be able to sense my advanced wretchedness.

•

"I wonder that a soothsayer doesn't laugh whenever he sees another soothsayer," Cicero said, or so I've heard, though probably not in English, likely in Latin, and with that I think that the wretch's advantage is, possibly, that he doesn't start crying when he sees another wretch, another poor beggar. I'm moved, affected, gripped more quickly, when I think of myself as a wretch than when I, for example, see other wretches come into The Hills. I get easily annoyed by other wretches. There, I said it. But I allow my own wretchedness to affect me. It's because I know a lot (but not everything) about the causes of my own wretchedness. And if I think about these reasons—something I should by no means do here—I can see that I have clear reasons for being a wretch, and the thought of these reasons, which have led to flaws in me, can move me in a second if I bring them up. I might think that it's not my fault I've become wretched, and feel that it's unfair that I have these shortcomings. But if I see another wretch, then all I see is that wretch. I don't see their flaws. I definitely don't see the sure-to-be-moving and unfair causes of his or her wretchedness. I just see the wretchedness and think that he or she should get a grip. He or she needs to pull themselves together and not be so miserable. *We all have our problems,* I think. *Now make sure you pull yourself together.* I stand, stooped, and think this. *Pull yourself together,* I think in my stoopedness, about another person; I think it coldly and without any compassion, at the very sight of someone radiating one kind of misery or another. I can stand there, completely crazed inside, stooped and crooked over my own faults and gaps, internal wounds which never heal, which split open at the slightest irregularity or reminder. I can stand like that, utterly cold, and be irritated by a *wretched* fellow human and their faults, their cracks, and their crookedness.

SCROLL

WIDOW KNIPSCHILD HAS TOTTERED OVER TO HER
table and pointed to a crumble; I have placed it in front of her, followed by a dessert spoon which I put down, gentle as a cat's paw,
above the pie plate. Gray, subdued, and pale colors are the common thread, if I may say so, linking Widow Knipschild's outfit.
She is as colorless as ash, Widow Knipschild. I've always liked her.
Elegant lady. Intelligent being. She was a professor in cultural history in her day. "You know," she once said. "You know I worked
at Plantin-Moretus alongside my studies in Antwerp?" I knew it;
she had told me before, in her senile way. "You know, back then
we actually snuck in to print pamphlets on the old printing presses
at night?" That I didn't know. "I printed my first pamphlet on the
oldest press there, which, as you might have heard, is the second
oldest preserved printing press on earth. And it's still in the place
where it has always been, since a handful of years after Gutenberg.
You can see it on the floor; its feet have eaten into the woodwork."

"Fantastic," I said. "Do you know what the first leaflet I printed said?" No, how could I have known that? "It said, 'The great are only great because we are on our knees. Let us rise. Proudhon.'" "You don't say," I said, surprised, following up with a question about whether she did the printing with the old lead they have at the museum. "Oh yes," she said then. "What else?" And then she cut a piece of the pear tart I had placed in front of her, light as an eiderdown, and spent a long time tasting it before she finished: "The reason I'm always here at The Hills is because it's the place in Oslo—well, perhaps even the whole of Scandinavia—which reminds me most of Plantin-Moretus." "That might be laying it on thick," I said. "No it isn't," said Widow Knipschild. "It's how it is. This is the place for the long lines."

•

I said that I never use my phone during working hours, but that's gone a bit off the rails today. From time to time I have to check for news from Edgar, or possibly from Anna. It might be too early to expect a message, but what if they've sent one? I try to sneak past the chef, but it's in vain. The passage between his rounded back and the blackened, greasy, pan-covered wall on the way to the cramped wardrobe corner where my all-weather jacket is hanging is so narrow that it feels like a sexual act to squeeze through there. The chef is frying mushrooms and onions; he's literally throwing the mushrooms and onions around in the frying pan. He tosses the mushrooms and onions with firm flicks, and in between they, the mushrooms and onions, fly high in the air, almost a meter above the pan, or that's how it seems. He glares at the mushrooms and onions when they're at eye level. The mushrooms and onions hang in the air in front of his face. Then they fall, the slices of mushroom and slivers of onion, all together, back into the frying pan. Accompanying this tossing of vegetables are sharp elbow movements, his lower arm is moving back and forth like the piston of a locomotive, and I'm immediately concerned about passing behind him. What if I bump? I clear my throat. The chef pauses. A sign that I can pass. The mushrooms and onions are sizzling, I have to hurry before they burn. He cooks at high temperatures, the chef.

Anna has sent zero messages, and there's not a peep from Edgar. It's only a little after ten. When will Anna arrive? I wonder. I use the two-handed, straight-arm phone technique typical of old people. The phone is in my left hand while a crooked finger pads across the glass like a dry croissant. I don't even understand how the phone can react to my jabbing fingertip. I watch some videos produced by drones while I'm in here, inside, out there, online. You have to deal with a lot of drone recordings nowadays. These drones have recorded crystal clear images of a tank attack in the Jobar district of Damascus. Down in the bathroom, here at the restaurant, there has long been a beautiful pattern of black-and-white stone on the floor. The black stones are possibly dark green. Or are they more blue? Oxford blue, verging on black? In any case, the repeated dark and white pattern reminds me of the old Damascus. The drone images in my feed show a Damascus which looks, more than anything, like Widow Knipschild's crumble. Nothing but sand-colored grains and lumps. The oldest continuously inhabited city in the world, as it's known by some, that's what I'm seeing here, completely in ruins. I scroll a little more. That can't be illegal. Now I see an image of a girl standing on the hooves of a horse which is lying on its back, a bit like a dog. A cat that says "cock." A hand being chopped off, Islamist style. An article about the relationship between screen radiation and the yellowing of teeth. What do you know. My teeth are fairly white. Maybe it's because of my limited screen time, in combination with my healthy skepticism of technology? An unexpected bonus. Why, and not least *how*, would Anna have sent me a message at ten past ten? Using phones is bound to be forbidden at school—not that I know anything in particular about that. The agreement is clear. She'll come here when she's finished. Why would she bother texting? Does she even have a phone? And Edgar is probably on a plane or busy in his important meeting. The urgent business, as he called it. I send him a quick message:

THE MYSTERIES OF THE BRAIN AND THE HEART REVEAL THEMSELVES IN THE SMALL, REMARKABLE, AND UNEXPECTED COMBINATION OF LETTERS AND WORDS. YOU LEECH.

After that, I scroll a bit further. I see a puma looking after a tiny frog, a dwarf frog. A 105-year-old tells us that it might not be worth spending your entire life on a strict diet, free from processed meat, since the last thirty years are doomed to be repetitive and joyless anyway. I also see a girl wearing Idi Amin's uniform, a copy down to the very last detail, for Halloween. She looks quite like him. A she–Amin in miniature.

"Hey," I hear the chef say outside. Is it me he's talking to as I stand here, besotted with my phone?

"Sorry?"

"They're calling for you."

I shove my telephone back into my all-weather jacket before I expose myself in the most embarrassing way by having to squeeze past the chef. I strut into the restaurant with flared nostrils and scrolled-out eyes. The florist has cut the stamen from the lilies, OK, but what about the colored kale from Thursday? Has he forgotten about that? The colored kale, or ornamental kale, as the florist calls it, has started to smell. I catch a *hint* of rotten ornamental kale. There's a sharp *note* in the air, tormenting us. Widow Knipschild sits in the middle of all that, shrouded in her own cloud of perfume, which, for her, certainly curbs the awful smell of stale ornamental kale, but it's not her who needs my attention. And nor is it the beer-drinking actor. It's the Maître d'.

"Tables seven and twelve need serving," he says firmly.

"Of course," I say, looking at him without yielding, as I've learnt to do, despite my natural lack of authority: this confrontational staring back at someone is my talent. I might be completely in pieces on the inside, but to stand there with a waiter's idiotic and equally impenetrable "pride" staring back—well, that I can do. I don't give in. I use my face to say *Of course* back at the Maître d's face. The Maître d's face is shiny with lotion. He has a kind of broken wet look going on there, combined with his dry hair. Isn't it supposed to be the other way round?

"And please do something about that kale."

"The florist was just here. Should I call him back?"

"What do you need the florist for?"

"To sort out the kale."

The Maître d' rubs his eyes. It looks completely grotesque. How can he put pressure on those bags without bursting them?

"What do you mean?" he says wearily.

"It's not good floristry to leave the *Brassica* from Thursday, standing there smelling like death and manure," I say. "He should fix it."

The Maître d' continues his rubbing, to my horror, while his left hand points dejectedly towards the bar. The Romanesco is lying there. Ugh.

"There's a lot of the stuff in here," he says.

"Ah . . . of course," I say, *jolting* towards the Romanesco as though I had been given a rap behind the knees. "The Romanesco. I'm so sorry."

"It was the young lady who drew my attention to it," he says quietly, nodding his head in the direction of the Child Lady, who is still sitting over by the curtain.

" 'It'?"

"That you had left behind the vegetable."

"Ah, you don't say," I say, grabbing the Romanesco with both hands, simultaneously feeling myself derail. "What did she say?"

"She said that you left the cauliflower—the cabbage."

"I understand."

"It's good that you understand."

"But what did she say?"

"What do you mean?"

"How did she say it?"

"How did she say it? By opening her mouth, I should think."

"I see. But how could you know it was me she meant?"

The Maître d' stops his rubbing and lets his hand drop like a lead weight. He stands there for a few seconds with his eyes closed, as though he is sleeping upright. Then—with some kind of facial exertion which begins with him raising his eyebrows to lift his heavy lids upwards and continues with him opening his mouth wide to also pull them downwards—he finds a gap between lid and bag so that he can start his repetitive blinking/squinting and slowly bring his surroundings into focus, not unlike a mammal opening its eyes for the very first time.

"There was no misunderstanding," he says, gaping.

"Of course not," I say.

". . ."

"But she can't have named me."

" 'Well, let's see!' said the blind man to the deaf one," he says with satirical enthusiasm.

He doesn't need to do that to me.

The very tip of the Romanesco is pointing towards the raised seat where the Child Lady was sitting before she moved, towards the barstool, which is a raised seat; that's where it's pointing. Vanessa hurries by with her dutiful stride, and I seize the opportunity to delegate.

"Hey!" I shout a bit too harshly. Vanessa jumps. "Can you call the florist?"

"Wasn't he just here?"

"Sadly, he didn't do his job."

"I'll call him, then," Vanessa says, scratching the stubble on her head.

ANNA ARRIVES

HERE COMES BLAISE ENGELBERT, VIGOROUSLY, through the curtain. Engelbert has a *whiff* about him. He's really dressed up today. What a suit. We're all used to seeing quality suits in here, but this one is spectacular. The cut. The materials. Sharper than patterned Damascus steel. That might be a metaphor from the wrong cultural context, but it's all the same. If you can imagine translating British tailoring to traditional Syrian metalwork, well, then you can picture Blaise Engelbert right now—he's as sharp as damascened metal. I've never seen anything like it. Even the Maître d' gives him a quiet but unmistakable compliment, and that isn't something you see every day.

"I have to say . . . ," I say as he passes.

"Yes," Blaise says. He knows what I'm referring to.

"Yeah, that's really something," I say abstractly.

"Yup," says Blaise.

I think you have to be my age to put a value on lapels like that.

It's as though children—with all their hypersensitivity to food and that kind of thing—don't take in the important details. Children don't notice the small things. How a glowing light in the corner of a room can mean so infinitely much. How a good or bad chair can save or ruin an interior. And the opposite: how relaxed your sensory apparatus becomes by the time you're my age. I never get carsick. I can eat moldy cheese and rotten fish. I can chomp on calluses and fibers without retching. I couldn't do that as a child. There can be as many lumps as you like in the soup. I can knock back schnapps without pulling a face. That's impossible for children. But if the door is ajar and I feel the slightest draft around my feet, the faintest hint of cold, well, then I react. I react powerfully. *Which door is open now?* I wonder. As a child, I could wear wet shoes for hours without noticing. I would smell like sheep when I came in again, my thick wool socks would be so wet. My nails cracked, but I didn't realize until it was too late. I wouldn't have noticed Blaise Engelbert's masterful lapels as a nine-year-old, either. They would have been invisible to me. But now his lapels are all I can see. *How about those lapels? No, I've never seen anything like them.*

The Child Lady jumps up from the marble table as though everything were choreographed, and follows Blaise over to table ten, my table. It's time for the pulling out of chairs now. The Child Lady gives Blaise her hand. Blaise takes it gallantly. I take hold of the back of the chair I assume the Child Lady will be sitting in and pull it out while I indicate with my other hand where she can/should/will/must sit down: *Here, on the chair I have pulled out.*

"Thank you," she says.

"Of course," I say.

She moves so that the backs of her knees are in front of the seat and the fronts of her thighs against the edge of the table, waiting for me to push in the chair. I catch a slight hint of musk again. It is musk, isn't it? She is waiting for the touch of the seat against the backs of her knees as a sign that she can strain her thigh muscles—the front group, the so-called four-headed muscle, the body's biggest— and then bend her knees to sink down onto the chair, likely with a complex interplay of tightening in the frontal and medial thigh muscles, supported by her hamstrings to the back, so that she is squatting slightly for a moment, with the great gluteus muscle, the gluteus maximus, fully tensed, waiting for me to push the chair be- neath her, which I do, so that she can comfortably sit down.

"There," she says.

I see thousands of possibilities for how I can parry this "There," but I steer myself away from saying "Voilà," "So, there, now," "Excellent," or anything else stupid. I control myself and I breathe repeatedly through my nose, down into my mustache. Sensibly quiet, that's how I keep myself. Professionally and sensibly quiet.

Apropos of controlling yourself—or the counterpoint of control, letting loose—I must say that Old Johansen took the change of mood seriously. The music on the mezzanine is *presto* now, so to speak. It's *vivace* on that raised, enlarged, ingrown bay of his, or is it called *vivo*? Is it *vif* the French call this kind of quick, cheery music, verg- ing on the hectic? Is it a bit lively? What does the Maître d' think about that? Don't we, the staff, in our jackets, black-and-white, take on a slightly comical character when accompanied by this *lebhaft* music? I wish he would dampen the mood a touch, Johansen.

There's something about that musky scent. It smells a bit like old lady. On a young woman like the Child Lady, it becomes utterly special. Blaise also uses fragrance, and it's extremely subtle. His scent mixes with the Child Lady's soft musk. What does Blaise use? There's a hint of Grey Vetiver, but the wood note is different, the wood in his scent is closer to Encre Noire. More aquilaria, or oud. You can detect a damper type of wood than in the Vetiver. Does he mix scents? Very few men do. Is Blaise so advanced? He probably is. I almost feel high on these scents now. A cheerful mix of smells, like Anna talked about. That's the kind of advancement we want here at The Hills. In here, we want unexpected combinations and mixes of the highest, best qualities. We want, figuratively speaking, eggs to be plucked from hens, and for the paste of crushed and ground sun-flower seeds to be pressed until the oil runs out, and for this oil to be mixed with the egg and whipped hard, so that the whole thing changes character and becomes *mayonnaise*. That's what we want, like I said, figuratively speaking. Blaise's and the Child Lady's scents have an almost magical effect when mixed, equivalent to the mir-acle of mayonnaise. Something completely new and special occurs between them, between their aromas, their bouquets. (How to de-scribe mayonnaise to someone who has only tasted sunflower seeds and eggs on their own?)

Through the window, I notice that the Pig is being driven to the door, in a car that can't be described as anything but *a ride*. It's exactly 1:30, his usual time. I show the Pig to the table where Blaise is already glittering in his suit, with the Child Lady glowing by his side.

"Are we expecting anyone else?" I ask, bobbing up and down on my toes.

"Just the three of us," says the Pig.

"Three it is." I begin to clear away the fourth setting. "Can I tempt you with anything before your food?"

"I'll risk a glass of the white burgundy."

"Wonderful."

I place the white burgundy in front of the Pig's hand, light as a soap bubble. He nods in thanks and touches the crystal, runs his index finger, all dry, and his thumb, all stumpy, rough, up and down the stem. Then he solemnly lifts the glass and sips. The Child Lady glances upwards, as though she were twelve years old and I were a friend of her father's and she were the Pig's daughter and the Pig were my friend. Her smile is delivered with a closed mouth at first, but then she parts her lips. It's like a curtain being raised from her much-discussed dental arch. The Child Lady gives me the whole row of pearly whites; her smile crushes everything else around it.

•

It's approaching a quarter to two. The time of day when children Anna's age finish school, I think. Or is it? Does she go to any kind of clubs? After-school activities? If Edgar had given me a time, I would have been able to avoid falling into speculation around Anna's arrival. I quickly squeeze past the chef and into the wardrobe corner. Zero messages from Anna. Nothing from Edgar. Once again, I'm staring at a blank screen. A bit of scrolling can't be prohibited. First I see a picture of SpongeBob balancing two corn on the cobs, one on each eyeball, plus a '90s recording of Eminem rapping about pickles as he fries onion rings in Detroit. I also learn that Jewish families who fled from the Nazis back in the day are now seeking German passports because of conditions in the UK. Damn Edgar.

•

Vanessa, with her close-cropped hair, traipses over with the florist. He's behind her, in his florist's uniform, which is essentially a gardener's outfit: working clothes. Robust trousers with a set of functional pockets. A pair of gloves sticking out of one. Now I have to grill him a little. We don't want any stench in here.

"Hey!" I say, with my characteristic lack of timing. "Florist!" I blurt out.

The florist reacts. As does the Maître d', who is standing over by table seventeen. He looks at me like a deep-sea anglerfish, with bulging eyes and an unhappy mouth, the wall lamp sticking out from a panel just to the left of his face like one of those antennae with a glowing lump that those fishes have.

"One moment," I say, holding my fingers in the air while I move my left hand, with the bandage, behind my back.

The florist leans against the bar and studies my walk over to him. My footsteps clomp against the pretty mosaic floor. He can watch my head movements, the hen-like motion, the strutting. The stoop. I wonder whether I'll manage to keep up the momentum.

"Hey," I say.

"Yes?"

"The colorful kale."

"The decorative kale, yes."

"Do you notice it?"

"Do I notice it?"

I flare my nostrils and sniff gently with my big nose, plus I give a brief wave with one hand to signify odor.

"Do you notice the kale?" I repeat.

"Can't you just tell me what you want?"

"It stinks."

"Then you need to take it out," says the florist.

"Well, you can carry it out, then."

"I was up at Høybråten," says the florist. "Did you make me drive all the way back here just to carry a withered plant outside?"

I take hold of his upper arm, not too hard but firmly, and lead him towards Blaise and the Child Lady. We stop two meters from their table. I draw in more air through my nostrils to signal that he should do the same. "Smell," I say. The florist sniffs cautiously.

I tell him that this is the scentscape we aim for at The Hills. Oud. Aquilaria. Mixed with gastronomic aromas. The scentscape? The florist looks confused. Now I pull him over to the bar, where there is a huge arrangement of musty decorative kale. "Not this," I say. He asks whether I'm serious. Yes, you can bet your life I am. I ask him to inhale. Honestly, says the florist. Your work, or lack of it, I continue, has disturbed the scent panorama. You need to en-sure smooth blooming. The florist tries to explain that plants don't have an expiry date. If something withers between Monday and Friday, surely we can just take it out? Like I said, I say again, and with a police commissioner's movement, I grip his arm, but with the wrong hand—the bandage twists and the blister stings. I try to swap, but in my fumbling the florist snatches his arm away and says Don't touch me. He pulls back and shakes his head irritably. I try to grab him but just end up shoving his shoulder with an awkward right hand.

"Stop it," he says, moving with tetchy, floristic steps towards the exit. I'm knocked off-kilter, off balance, tilted. Then he disap-pears behind the curtain. The florist is not happy now. I wonder whether he'll ever be back to do his floristry—or de-floristry, if you can put it like that—here at The Hills.

And, as if that wasn't enough, as I'm standing there, star-ing after the raging florist, two small hands appear and part the curtains by the entrance. Anna peers in. Here she is. My insides jump. She bends down. A good bucket height above her head, an outstretched shirt sleeve appears. The curtain moves to one side. Who does this bony hand belong to? My insides jump and jump. Anna takes a step forward, and in comes Sellers, tall as he is. Bewitching as he is. The scamp is standing in the doorway. On his face, he is wearing the biggest smile of all, as is fitting for a scamp.

"Sweet girl," he says to me with a wink.

PART V

HOLBEIN

THEY SAY THAT HANS HOLBEIN THE YOUNGER'S sketched portrait of Baron Wentworth is damaged and doesn't bear Holbein's distinct left-handed hatching, Blaise says eagerly. They say that the drawing may have been tampered with at a later date. The hat and the ear are flat as a pancake, fair enough, and the head of hair could certainly be called uninspired. The dirty ink spot giving the right eye definition against the brim of the hat is certainly a later addition. But everyone who has had this drawing before them, says Blaise—and now he puts his shoulder to the wheel to carry his audience, Sellers, with him, and spells it out with emphasis—everyone who has seen this drawing one-on-one, live, with their own eyes, knows that it's first-rate.

Blaise says all this to Sellers, shamelessly, standing by Sellers's table, table thirteen, gesticulating, with the Pig by his side. He is speaking loudly enough for me to hear everything as I hide here, bowed, with a heavy face, behind the pillar, waiting for a sign. They'll probably seal the deal with something to eat or drink soon. That's how adults behave.

The facial hair beneath Wentworth's nose, Blaise continues, is comparable in terms of genius to the way Sir Thomas Wyatt's mustache is depicted—no more, no less. The contouring on the bridge of his nose is formidable. *Exceptional.* That bridge is second to none. Literally. It's on a level with the highlights of Velázquez's Pope Innocent X's lower lip, says Blaise. And I mean that, he says. Big words, but that's the way it is. The coloring on Wentworth's nose and nostrils, which is impossible to capture in reproductions, is so subtle, so delicate and über-minimal, that there's no equal. Taken as a whole, including the clumsiness of the hat, the feather, and the shadow from the brim, the drawing is a mystery. As with many of Holbein's Tudor drawings, it's difficult to say when, and by whom, the ink contours were added, if not by Holbein himself. Were they applied in order to transfer the image to woodblock or canvas? The silver point—when was that added? The brushwork ranges from masterful to simple. The mediocre ear and the sublime depiction of how the lace collar bends around Wentworth's neck—how can these two levels be found on the same sheet of paper? None of Holbein's drawings contain more contradictions than the sketch of Wentworth, and they raise one another to the highest of artistic heights. At the same time, the drawing is vanishingly faint. Almost invisible.

"And what's the point here?" Sellers wants to know.

"Well, it's that I want you to come and take a look at the draw-ing," says Blaise, still wearing his spectacular suit jacket.

"I have it at home," he adds.

"That can't be true," says Sellers.

"Yes, come with me and you'll see," says Blaise.

"No, lay off it," says Sellers.

But Blaise smiles triumphantly and nods slowly. "You know, Holbein's Tudor drawings aren't framed in the library at Windsor. They're in an acid-free box. In a pile. Some have passe-partout, others don't. But we can't talk about that out here," says Blaise. "We can smooth out the details at my place," he says quietly.

"No, that's a bit much," says Sellers. "That needs digesting. We need a bit of cheese for that."

He shouts: "Roll out the cheese!"

Blaise nods and waves intensely in my direction. Time for the trolley! With a bit of cheese, they'll celebrate that contact has been established. We have a three-tier cheese trolley. The tiers present a selection of cheeses, and on top there are two copper pots contain-ing, respectively, walnuts in a red wine reduction and a compote.

•

To recap Anna and Sellers's entrance once more: Sellers held the curtain for Anna and allowed her to slip in ahead of him. Smiling, he walked behind her to his usual table. He gave me a quick hello, as he usually does, as I stood there welcoming him, before the shock came: Sellers shouted a "Hey there!" as he passed the Child Lady's table, where the Pig and Blaise were also sitting. The Child Lady said hello back, and the two men nodded politely.

And with that, the contact between tables ten and thirteen was a fact, I thought to myself. Everything is going just as the Pig planned. He's pleasant and sociable, the Pig, but he's sly, I've always said that. So sly, so sly. He has deliberately used the Child Lady to get to Sellers. He used me at first, trying to get hold of me to talk about this and that, then he turned to the Child Lady. The Child Lady is the perfect collaborator.

After that, no more than five or six minutes passed before the Child Lady sat down at table thirteen, Sellers's seat of honor, where he sat enthroned. Conversation flowed. She touched Sellers on his forearm as she laughed. There was gesturing towards the Pig's table. The Pig and Blaise were like two glowing lightbulbs. Then she was spinning an invisible thread between the two tables, two otherwise separate worlds, tables ten and thirteen. The Child Lady gestured for the Pig and Blaise to come over. And before you knew it, Blaise and the Pig were standing by table thirteen in their fancy suits, talking about the Holbein until Sellers couldn't believe his own ears. "It can't be true," Sellers said. "What a joke."

It was discussed back and forth for a good fifteen minutes after that. And then they wanted cheese. And as I now push the cheese trolley over to table thirteen, Blaise and the Pig have cause to sit down. Standing behind the trolley, slicing a piece of Comté for Blaise, a piece of Port Salut for Sellers, and so on while they discuss whether it's a real or fake Holbein that Blaise is meant to have at his place—as the Child Lady gives the otherwise hobo-like table a glow—I find the experience humiliating. I don't know why, but I really do.

"A bit of the Reblochon, too," Blaise says in mid-chomp. "I really like cow. Don't you prefer cow?"

"Yes, so long as it's smear-ripened," says the Pig.

"Port Salut is smear-ripened, God help me," says Sellers. "And I should think it's cow?" He glances at me with equal measures questioning, mocking, and alcohol in his eyes.

"The Port Salut is made from cow's milk," I confirm.

"I'll take a bit of chèvre," the Child Lady says with a chuckle. She is a complete and utter consumer. And that's how the first hour passes.

•

In that hour, Anna has been doing her homework, with hairclips at her temples and a plait at the back, her rucksack by the side of the classic marble top. Who plaits her hair in the morning? I jumped when she came in, even though I had been waiting for her all day. Yes, I really jumped.

"Go over to your table, Anna," I said a bit too loudly, striding out into the kitchen and hurrying back with four kinds of sausage arranged on a plate, which I placed in front of her as light as an autumn leaf. "You can enjoy these sausages before dinner."

"Thanks."

"Would you like anything to drink?"

"Just water."

"No apple juice? We have the good one from Abildsø."

"No thanks. It's a bit floury."

"Oh? I think it's both delicate and tasty."

"I think I'll have water."

"Then water you shall have."

Anna pulled out her schoolbooks. I poured water. At table thirteen, they were wolfing down their cheese. They quaffed the dessert wine I thoughtfully recommended. The mood is now worryingly jovial. Sellers really is in his element. He's doling out his pickpocket-like charm. And, as expected, he'll want a nip of something strong. He raises his arm and waves. The others at the table are on board. They want a snifter, too. It's half past five, but they want shots already. The Pig, Blaise, and the Child Lady nod when Sellers suggests they should all have one.

"Anna," I say on my way over to the bar, to the alcohol.

"Yes?"

"I've got something to show you."

"Oh."

"Have you finished your homework?"

"Almost, I just have maths to do."

"What kind of maths is it?"

"Division with decimals."

"I've almost forgotten how to do that."

"It's OK."

"Is it without a calculator?"

"Everyone can divide with a calculator."

". . ."

"Give me a wave when you've finished, and I'll show you something."

"OK."

"Oh, also?"

"Yes?"

"Do you have a phone?"

"No."

"Do you know when your dad is coming?"

"No, but I guess he'll just come here," says Anna.

"Yes, I suppose he will."

I signal *Four snifters* to the Bar Manager and slope off towards the kitchen. Where's the Romanesco? Has the chef seen the Romanesque cauliflower? Yes, he uses his knife to point to the counter, where it's lying with the quince and something else green. I grab the vegetable with both hands and notice as I do that the bandage around my blister is slack and disgusting. I'll have to change it. With an "Excuse me," I squeeze past the chef and into the wardrobe corner. Nothing from Edgar. I send him a message.

ANNA IS DOING HER HOMEWORK. BEEN HERE A GOOD HOUR. HOW ARE YOU GETTING ON?

The logic, Edgar often says, is that life in the big city is so sad that we may as well sell it for money. But no one earns from his lack of punctuality. I leave the bandage as it is and squeeze back past the chef to serve the shots to table thirteen. Sellers knocks his back practically before I've even put it down. The others follow suit. They immediately order another round. One snifter rarely remains one. Anna waves to me. She has finished her maths.

"Did you manage it?" I say.

"Yes, of course."

"I want to show you something fun."

With a finger in front of my face, meant to illustrate *Look*, I bring the Romanesco from behind my back and gently place it on the marble tabletop in front of her. She looks at it, then at me. I explain that it's a Romanesque cauliflower. "Isn't it very special?"

"Yes," Anna agrees. I laugh friendly, but my laugh is like a brief honk of an air horn, more aggressive than disarming.

"You can draw this to pass the time." Anna nods.

Then I launch into my speech about fractals and Mandelbrot, just like I did with the Child Lady. Anna listens. She asks who M. C. Escher is. "Well, let me tell you," I say, continuing to teach. "And that's not all," I proceed. "It tastes great. And it's healthy. If you like, I can ask the chef to steam it for you, so you can have it for dinner. Draw first and eat later," I say, followed by a quick honk of the horn.

Anna nods and nods.

WAX CRAYON

THE BAR MANAGER WANTS TO TALK. SHE'S REACTING to the gathering at table thirteen. "What kind of event is this?" she wants to know.

"It's something about them wanting Sellers to follow them home and look at a drawing," I say.

"That seems unlikely," says the Bar Manager. "Why? A valuation? In that case, it's Raymond they should be asking. Sellers has no idea."

"But Raymond always comes with that charlatan Bratland in tow," I say, "and no one wants him around. And with such an elegant girl as she, the young one, at the table, it's impossible to spend time with Bratland. He's always looking for a leg over. He's a perv. He's a phony."

The Bar Manager gathers that the Pig and Blaise have seized their chance now that Bratland isn't hanging on, for once.

I set a few tables. Tablecloths and underlays are smoothed. The crumber comes out. My eyes restlessly sweep the room. I take in everything. I really do. I know how far Anna has got in her draw‑ing of the Romanesco. I know which shots have or have not been drunk at table thirteen. The Child Lady seems restless. But she has nowhere to go now, does she? Everyone of interest is already sitting at table thirteen. What's next? My eyes are locked in a duel with the Maître d's; his eyes see everything mine see, and possibly even more. I mistakenly serve a roulade to a group at table eight. He points to the roulade and I carry it away before the group man‑ages to remark on my mistake.

"What should we make of this?"

"I'm sorry," I say.

"If you're born a penny, you'll never be a dollar," he says.

I can feel my right eye getting bloodshot.

•

Before I know it, the Child Lady is standing next to Anna, bent over her drawing. Damn that Child Lady; she's quick as a flash. Does Anna have to be dragged into this mess, too? Without blinking, I hurry over to them. "What's going on here?" I say, but my question just bounces off them. I don't have the authority to cut through.

The Child Lady doesn't even look up; she says to Anna: "When I was little, I had such a crazy number of projects on the go. I was completely in my own little world. I could sit for hours cutting out magazines."

Isn't that typical. The Child Lady talks with emotion about her childhood, to hint that she hasn't moved past it and has remained fundamentally naive. Now she puts her nail to the drawing, to a spot where Anna has missed something.

"I used to wash all the time," she says to Anna. "I declared war on microbes. I refused to hurry in the mornings." She giggles. "I declared war on time. I declared war on worry. I declared war on darkness. I declared war on quiet. I declared war on fat." Anna continues to draw. "And then I declared war on war," the Child Lady says, looking at me.

"So I'm not the only one to be served this handsome cauliflower?"

"Yes, Anna was going to try to draw it."

"I don't know if I can get any more of the detail," Anna says.

"It's a very nice drawing. I'll leave you two alone," says the Child Lady.

Anna waves to her.

"Too sweet!" the Child Lady says, waving back. "She's flirting with me. Are you flirting with me, Anna?"

This is verging on audacious. Anna isn't flirting. Children don't "flirt" the way mothers and women always claim that they do. It's the Child Lady doing the flirting. She flirts and seduces, even when she isn't trying to seduce anyone. There's something strange about the Child Lady. From a certain distance she looks like an angel, but close-up, like a devil. She goes back to Sellers's table and sits down by Blaise. Damn it, how to get rid of her?

"You've really captured the pattern, Anna," I say.

"But it's completely impossible."

"You've even drawn the lines showing how the endless pattern in the conical shape follows spiral formations inwards and inwards. I think it's fantastic, Anna."

The Child Lady forces herself back into the conversation at table thirteen. I don't know what I should say about her appearance over there. It seems like the simplest things are the most painful for the Child Lady. The most "human" are the most mechanical. The Child Lady is optimistic, positive, satisfied, enthusiastic, cheerful. In other words, she's suffering.

"Who was that lady?" Anna asks.

"Oh, she's Graham's friend. The dapper old man who's always at table ten."

"She smelled nice."

"Everything concrete in this world has disappeared between the Child Lady's butt cheeks, I've thought to myself," I say.

"He-he-he," Anna laughs. " 'The Child Lady'?"

"Yes, the Child Lady. Two minutes, and your dinner will be ready."

•

It's a bizarre scene that's playing out at Sellers's table. They're discussing the sketch, and Sellers seems very interested. But then, in some strange way, he manages to misunderstand by asking detailed questions about how the wax crayon has been applied to the paper. Blaise explains that Holbein didn't use *crayons*, of course. But Sellers keeps talking about it. Crayons are handy, he says. They're good for markings underwater. I've often bought crayons from Karmøy Diving Services. They've got a good selection and such reasonable twelve-packs. Blaise corrects him: The drawing has the faintest chalk coloring. That would be impossible to achieve with crayons. I don't even know if they had crayons back then, he says. Possibly oil pastels? I'm not talking about oil pastels, Blaise, says Sellers. Who in their right mind would say "Holbein" and "oil pastel" in the same sentence? What kind of nonsense is this? You can get wax crayons at Hansmark, too. Hansmark? asks Blaise. Yes, at Hansmark they stock the so-called LYRA pencil. They'll write on any surface. Even dusty, rusty, oily, or wet. They also have a sharpener built into the lid. I don't think we're on the same page right now, says Blaise. It sounds like you're talking about a work- man's pencil, says the Pig. It's unlikely that the paper back then would tolerate such tools, says Sellers. Did they glue the paper in the 1500s? No, I'm not sure about that, says Blaise. There you have it, says Sellers. You can never be absolutely certain. Should we have another round of shots? Yes, can do, says the Pig. He turns to the Child Lady. Are you drinking your shots? Shouldn't I? says the Child Lady? Of course! Then let's all drink, says Blaise. Yes, let's, says Sellers. Another round of shots here!

"Another round of drinks," I say.

"We want more," says Blaise. He's cheery.

"Snifters all round," says Sellers.

The Child Lady looks up.

"Could I have an Amaretto?" she says.

"Definitely," I say.

"Ah, spirits made from pistachio nuts are never wrong!" says Sellers. "Good choice."

"Pistachio?" says Blaise.

"Amaretto, the liqueur of nuts," says Sellers.

The poise the Child Lady displays as she sits between Sellers and Blaise is more like an accountant's than a dancer's. I stride behind the bar, humpbacked, and relay the Amaretto order. "Did he say pistachio?" asks the Bar Manager.

"He did," I say.

I carry Anna's lasagne with pecorino, the way she likes it, with green salad on the side, plus a cola, and the steamed Romanesco on its own plate. I say that the Romanesco is mostly for fun's sake. She doesn't have to eat the whole thing. No, she says, she wants to. Then she catches sight of the bandage.

"Have you hurt your hand?"

"Yes, I managed to give myself a horrible blister in the cellar."

"The bandage is dirty. Haven't you changed it?"

"No, it happened yesterday."

"I can help you after I've eaten," she says. "I've done first aid at school."

The cheese topping on the lasagne is scalding hot: Anna knows that, which is possibly why she tackles the Romanesco first. Or is she actually curious? It's nice that she shows interest in my ideas. She holds the fork like a stick and cuts off a bit of the cauliflower. It tastes nice, she confirms with a quick nod. I ask whether she wants any pepper sprinkled on her pasta dish. "Yes, please," she says. I fetch the biggest pepper mill to sprinkle it, the one she's always liked. The Maître d' catches me on my way back.

"We'll have to try not to make it as late today," he says.

"Sorry?"

"With the child."

"No, of course," I say.

"Only a scoundrel gives away more than he owns, you know."

One of the most important qualities for modern man, if that's a concept, is mastering excess, Edgar says. What if you don't have this quality? Then you're in a pickle. I'm not always so good at filtering or sorting the continual stream of things, this pressure. And the Maître d' really doesn't help by sending these bitter pills in my direction, making my ramparts crack. Can't I give the girl a sprinkling of pepper without him bothering me with these vibes? I go over to Anna and season her lasagne with three firm twists.

THE GAUZE
BANDAGE

AND THEY'RE AT IT AGAIN, AT TABLE THIRTEEN. SELLERS asks me to come closer. I half kneel to hear what he's saying. In surfing, there's something called a tuck knee. You push your knee sideways to achieve a lower center of gravity. The concept also works in skateboarding and snowboarding. I have tuck knee now. I hold the bandage behind my back. Let me put it like this: having tuck knee here at The Hills is different to riding a swell in the Pacific or along a concrete ditch in Santa Monica. Here at The Hills, tuck knee means awkwardness, not style. Subordination. Obedience. Possibly weakness.

"It's all getting a bit warped here, but could we order food?" he says.

"But you've already had cheese," I say.

"Then we'll have to think outside the box." He laughs with a deep, whistling smoker's cough.

Everything is on its head now. All is out of place. It's like a state of emergency in here. They had the cheese first. After the cheese, they want dinner. I hesitate. Sellers looks at me.

"We can manage it," he says.

"I'm sure we can," I say. "But can I just see to one quick thing before I take your orders? There's just one thing."

"Of course," says Sellers. "Do your thing."

I hurry over to Anna. She has just begun her lasagne. "Anna, can I interrupt you a minute?" Anna smiles. "Do you want to change the bandage on the blister now?"

"Sure," she says, with her characteristic lack of hesitation. She gets up. "Where?" she says.

"We'll have to go to the cellar to fetch more gauze bandage," I say. "Do you want to come? It's a very special cellar."

She does; with enthusiastic steps she walks ahead of me through the curtain, out the door, round the building, and over to the cellar hatch. It's as cold as always. It's been dark for some time now. The neon sign on the other side of the street makes my hands look alternatingly washed-out salmon pink and pale green. Anna seems excited as I fumble with the lock and key. I smile apologetically. Her face changes color.

•

I stand with my left foot on the bottom step and tell Anna to come down. "The stairs are really steep. You have to turn around and go backwards," I say.

Anna turns around and moves slowly, with her heels first. Her feet are well wrapped in a pair of oversized Moon Boots—she actually has the classic Moon Boots—and they look almost comically big on her thin, beanstalk legs.

"Moon Boots, Anna?" I say.

"Yes," she says.

My hand is ready, the healthy one, in case she falls, but I don't touch her. She finishes crawling down and peers around the cellar.

"Wow," she says. It's clear she has never seen anything like it. "Look at the wine barrels. Are they real?"

Once, a few years ago, I had to go to the doctor because I could hear a ringing sound in my ears. As the doctor asked me questions in his little room, I cast a daft glance at his computer screen.

"Face rising and falling," he had written. That rising and falling is happening to my face now, I suspect.

"How far back does it go?" Anna says.

"Far. I'm not sure."

It's not light enough for us to make it to the drawer section containing jute, gauze bandages, rags, towels, slings, spools, patches, doilies, aprons, decorative covers, and cloths; I'll have to find the switch for the bulb in the next section of corridor. Anna asks where the gauze bandage is. I think it's straight ahead and then round the corner to the right, the opposite way to the fruit, vegetables, and Romanesco. Two seconds and I'll switch on the other light. I fumble along the wall and twist a knob, but then the light goes on behind the steps. "That wasn't right," I say with a smile.

But Anna is gone. This is perilous. I can't see her. I'm standing with the back of my head against the cellar roof. Everything but the so-called poker face runs off me. In the mirror in the mornings, I see the violent decay ravaging what was once me. I imagine that same decay is also going on inside, in my brain, in my liver, in the erectile tissue of my penis. And definitely in my nervous system. The purely physical decay of the nerves can partly explain the relationship between youthful confidence and the fact that you become crushed by doubt as you grow older. Shouldn't it be the other way around? Shouldn't you become more confident in yourself as the years pass? I try to think positively. I see my tired, weary face in the mirror every day, and say to myself: *This is the youngest you'll look for the rest of your life.*

"Are the bandages on this side or the far side of the cuttings?" Anna shouts.

I hear a giggle.

"The far side," I say loudly.

It goes quiet. Then I hear a scraping sound. Then another long moment of silence.

A loud thud with a metallic clang makes me jump.

"Whoops!" I hear Anna say. "Sorry!"

"Should I come over?" I say.

"Just stay there."

There's a joke cough. Mumbling, followed by a gasp. More whispering. Then silence.

"Hello?" I say.

Another gasp. She's not crying? Now it's quiet again. Then I hear padding. Here she comes. The floor is covered in earth. Anna is carrying the gauze bandage in both hands. It's a big roll, the size of a Christmas brawn. Her smile is splendid. Perhaps it would be best to keep her down here where things stand still. I could close the hatch. Lock her up. Lock the Child Lady out.

"Come on, Anna," I say, shooing her up the stairs.

ORDERS REVERSED

I LEAD ANNA INTO THE DAMASCUS-LIKE MEN'S TOILET
so she can help me. I sit down on the toilet lid and unwind the
old bandage. The blister and the flap of skin are disgusting. Blood,
pus, and dirt have soaked into the material. Anna kneels down in
front of me and studies the flap. Concentrating, she starts to apply
the new bandage. She turns the big roll of bandage 180 degrees
with each layer, so that it spreads out in an impressive adder pattern from my palm. She moves her tongue from one corner of her
mouth to the other in concentration.

"Do you have a safety pin or bandage hook?" Anna says.

Her face is smooth but slightly purple beneath the eyes. A clear
sign of sleep deprivation. Ugh, Edgar's wantonness is affecting the girl.

"The bandage isn't self-adherent; it's old," she says.

"I just tied it yesterday," I say.

She takes one of the clips from her hair and fastens the end by
my wrist. I'm very impressed by her ingenuity.

"You really know your stuff."

"Yes, sir," says Anna.

"You must feel like having the rest of your lasagne now."

•

Sellers is smirking. The Child Lady slowly drifts in his direction. I can only think of abstract ways to describe her. She's the path we walk down to lose ourselves, I think now. She's not acting; she doesn't put on appearances. It's as though her image puts on *her*. The bandage is nice and tight. I feel a bit more energetic.

"Are we ready to order, then?" I say as I run my hand between the guests and give the tablecloth a good de-crumbing.

Sellers says that they might go with the main course now; they can look at the starters later. The Child Lady asks if the chef can prepare mushrooms again. Chanterelles, ideally, and she'd like to have some sheep polypores, too, if there are any. Actually, I think there are, I say. Both rapeseed oil and butter, she says. A few shallots. That's all. Well-done. Iron pan. The mushrooms can't be allowed to boil. That's routine in the kitchen, I say. Blaise applauds her order. Then he smacks his tongue gently, as though he still has Reblochon on the roof of his mouth and wants to see which main will best follow the cheese, an absurdity in itself. He decides on an Italian steak from the daily menu which I, reliably, have chalked up on the board. Blaise pronounces *vitello alla Sarda* with impressive intonation; he wants it served traditionally and with potatoes—and peas, actually—to the side of the spinach, the chanterelles, and sauce.

With a refined hand gesture, the Pig indicates that it's Sellers's turn, but Sellers says that the Pig can order. No, after you, says the Pig. No, you first, Sellers insists. But when the Pig says "Grouse," Sellers quickly says "Plaice" over him, making their words blend together.

"Pardon?" I say.

The Pig tries "Grouse" again, but Sellers's timing is perfect; this time he says "Kid" over the Pig's order, mixing everything up. Sorry, you go first. The Pig smiles. No, you first, of course, Sellers says with a subordinate hand gesture. The Pig peers through his varifocal glasses and down at the menu and pretends to be reading it once more.

"Could I have . . ."

He runs a dry finger beneath the grouse dish. Blaise nods approvingly to the Child Lady.

"Hmmm . . . ," says the Pig.

He draws it out, peers at Sellers over the rims of his spectacles, then he gets ready. "G—" he says.

"T—" says Sellers, like a flash of lightning.

The Pig tries a feint.

"Gr—"

"Ta—" Sellers quickly says.

". . ."

"Grouse for Graham, tartare for Sellers," I say, not siding with either of them.

"Could I have the Worcestershire sauce in an egg cup to one side?" says Sellers.

"Of course."

"And do you have the chives from the chef's mother's garden?"

"I think that's what he always uses," I confirm.

"Could you ask him *not* to use those?"

"Absolutely," I say.

"The soil in the chef's mother's garden is affected by her living right by the racetrack," Sellers says quietly to the table. "The chives taste stale."

Sellers wants a beer with his tartare, but he butts in and corrects Blaise's French as Blaise orders a burgundy.

"There's more emphasis on the *u*," he says. "Burgúndy."

"OK, so you mean Bourgogne?" Blaise says.

"Indeed, more [buʁ]-gogne," says Sellers.

"Yes, I agree with that," says Blaise. "If you have the [gɔɲ] at the end there. So [buʁgɔɲ]."

"Yes, but you can't be sloppy with the *ú*. We're practically talking *ö*."

"That's where I fall short."

AMLOST OVER

I MANAGE TO MAKE THE CHEF'S COPPER PANS RATTLE
horribly when I go to check for messages from Edgar. The screen
is still black. My head feels tight. Anna can't sit here forever, plus
she's tired. Maybe a bit of scrolling will help dampen the unease? A
bird gets its beak caught in an emo's piercing. The urban myth that
Abraham Lincoln, John F. Kennedy, and Martin Luther King Jr.
were all shot at ten past ten is false, I read here. Lincoln was shot at
quarter past and didn't die until early the next morning. Kennedy
was killed at half past twelve, in the very middle of the day. Martin
Luther King Jr. was shot at one minute past six in the evening
and pronounced dead at five past seven. The fact that watches in
advertisements are always set to ten past ten is purely aesthetic, not
mythical, I learn. Shockingly, the next thing to appear is a picture
of Edgar. He is smiling next to someone in a dark suit, along with
an older gentleman with an outstanding bald head. To one side is a
woman who looks like what Michelle Obama would have looked

like if she were Slavic. Someone uploaded the picture half an hour ago. Doesn't that look like Copenhagen in the background? It's not Oslo, at any rate.

YOU AREN'T STILL IN COPENHAGEN?

The spire in the background might be Sankt Andreas Kirke. I can't hold back from leaving a comment beneath the picture, anonymously. *The kids' programs are amlost over,* I write. I notice the spelling mistake too late. *Amlost.* That's out there for anyone to read now. I'm the internet's most useless troll. It's well past seven, so it's going to fill up in here within the hour. There are limits to how much attention I can give Anna over the evening. Edgar needs to reply. I post a new message, anonymously. *I see you online in Copenhagen,* I write. Another misjudgment. Online and Copenhagen are, strictly speaking, two different places.

Anna is sitting at her table; she's reading sweetly, now with four clips in her hair, not five. I look at her with out-scrolled eyes. The colorful book cover suggests more fantasy. She has almost eaten up her Romanesco. I explain that Edgar isn't replying right now, so there'll probably be a bit more of a wait. She doesn't seem to mind. "Are you tired?" I ask. "Not really," she says, but her eyes tell a different story. I offer to get her some of the chef's twine so she can finger-weave a potholder or something. She says she's fine reading her book.

The Maître d' is hunched over the reservation protocol. "The table where the girl is sitting is reserved from 7:30," he says. "How long is she going to be here?" I reply that, unfortunately, I don't know. He asks whether I'm responsible for her. "I suppose I am," I say. "When poverty comes in at the door, love jumps out of the window," he says, and turns away. I ask what he means by that. After 8 p.m., I'll have to find somewhere else for her, he says. I head off to the bar to fetch the drinks for Sellers's table. While the Bar Manager pours the burgundy, she tells me that Blaise and the Pig really are nagging Sellers now. And the Child Lady is contributing. It's not far to Blaise's place; I can be your wing girl, she said, the Bar Manager says. Wing girl? What kind of word is that? I don't know. They're insisting on Sellers following Blaise home. I zone out. My windpipe is tight now. Sellers is difficult, she says. He's incredibly gentle and accommodating, but he's also impossible to crack. The Bar Manager is fired up. I am cursing Edgar. Cursing Blaise. The Child Lady. Damn you all to hell.

NEST

THIS IS DRAGGING ON. I HAVE NO IDEA WHEN MY shift ends, thanks to Edgar. He's keeping me trapped here. I'm tired. He's also forcing me past the chef, into the wardrobe, to the phone in my all-weather jacket pocket, meaning I'm constantly having small doses of the loathsome present day forced on me. Nowness makes me unwell.

YOU REALLY NEED TO GET IN TOUCH NOW.

Edgar has, ironically, sat here himself, complaining about this intrusion, this stream of impressions. It's been said before, he's said to me, and it'll probably be said again, but right now, today, I feel that, under these conditions, it's enough. The transfer of information we're exposed to has never been more aggressive than it is today. No, there have never been more of these transmissions than there are today, and you can say the same of every day that passes, says Edgar. The necessary processing of impressions is no longer a possibility for me, Edgar has said. Today it's over-the-top. I can't swallow these streams anymore. It all became too much today. It's like wanting a glass of water and being given a bucketful to the face. The stream has never been stronger. Today the stream was too strong. Never have I been more stuffed than today, on this last day in the series of all days. The feed has never been shriller. It's completely crazy now. So shrill. So violent. These are Edgar's words. And now he himself is hovering out there, so to speak, online in Copenhagen, floating into the phone in my coat pocket and dragging me out there, but not even answering. It's just under half an hour until Anna has to leave the table.

I hear Sellers arguing that it's Raymond who is the art expert, that they can call Raymond for him to come along and give them a valuation. Raymond? the others ask. Yes, that whale who's often with me, says Sellers. The guy with the typically south-Scandinavian look. An enormous, classic south Scandinavian. Yes, they remember him. But they're not sure, since he's always with that third man, who is so harsh. Bratland? Sellers asks. Yes, Bratland, the others say. Then Sellers chuckles and says that Bratland is as meek as a lamb. No, they don't need to worry about him. He's just a bit blunt. It's typical of the south-Scandinavian way, says Sellers. I don't know if I want to let a rascal like that anywhere near the Holbein, says Blaise, gently but honestly. Rascal? Ha, no, Bratland is trustworthy. He's the involved type, says Sellers. He's been doing music, surfing, and other sad activities for years. He might seem a bit irritable, perhaps, but there's not a bad bone in him. He is a bit skeptical, however, about nicer establishments like this, says Sellers. Is that what they've noticed? Once, he was completely floored by a complex and much-too-big gourmet package. Bratland couldn't cope with it at all and completely broke down. The package arrived far too late in the evening, Sellers says, together with a side package, a wine package, which contained heavy red wine. It led to a night of agonizing toilet visits. His ambitions as a gourmand were shelved after that, and Bratland has since borne a grudge towards gourmandism. That's why he might seem a bit harsh towards everything that could be seen as snobby. Make of that what you will, says Sellers, but Bratland likes pre-prepared tacos best of all. He can't get enough of them. Do you have any opinions around the taco as a dish?

•

With that, the Maître d' is standing sternly by Anna's side, making sure she packs up her things—her little knapsack, I might have said, because it's a sorry sight. "Bag" or "satchel" are no longer suitable words for describing what Anna is being forced to pack, because she's packing her knapsack. I ask what on earth is going on, and the Maître d' says that time is up. Honestly, I say, the girl's father has been held up, and she has to stay until he gets here. One man's floor is another man's ceiling, the Maître d' says with his big, bloated face close to mine. Would you mind calming down with the sayings, I say. I'm flaring up inside. He continues to stare. Anna is standing with her knapsack ready, looking at us. Her face is slightly pale, I seem to notice. There's no doubt she's tired. What do I do now?

•

"Come and sit with us, Anna."

It's the Child Lady: here she is, circling, getting involved. Why is she butting in? She looks very sincere. But I think the Child Lady's true face is also a mask, and an awful one.

"We've got space over here!" she says. The Maître d' looks like he's had some kind of stroke.

"And we need our starters and aperitifs!" Sellers shouts. He holds his index finger in the air.

"We're ready for the starters!"

"See?" says the Child Lady. "Old Sellers is there, too. He misses you."

"Come here, my girl," Sellers says, letting his index finger drop and become a hook which he moves through the air, indicating that Anna should go over to him.

"Hey, Moon Boots!" the Child Lady says with a gasp.

"Yes," says Anna.

There's a seat next to the dashing Blaise. Anna places her knapsack against the chair and greets him sweetly. And the Pig, well-mannered, with her paw. Sellers leans across the table like an uncle and asks her if there was any awkwardness with the

Maître d' over there. Awkwardness, has there been awkwardness? he says. Not really, says Anna, nobly following up by saying that she does in fact understand why children aren't allowed to be here so late. No, don't listen to that puffer fish, Sellers whispers, puffing out his cheeks. Anna giggles. We'll get him moving now. Watch this, Anna, he says with a wink. Maître d'. Excuse me, Maître d'? The Maître d' turns around, full to the brim with stern, Protestant ethics—the general principle behind the capitalist machinery, as Edgar likes to claim—and nods doggedly. Sellers says that his "niece" would like to have profiteroles while the adults have their starters. The Maître d' purses his lips slightly as he takes the order.

"Now they're having starters," the Maître d' says, shocked, to the Bar Manager and me. How has this happened? Not easy to say. Sellers turned everything back to front, I mumble. He reversed their dinner. We just have to do it the wrong way round.

"The girl can stay awhile longer, but then that's it," the Maître d' commands, heading into the kitchen with his work-ethic stride, to pass on the order from table thirteen himself. "Lotion time," the Bar Manager mutters. And once the starters are ready, the Maître d' comes out and serves them himself, demonstratively. The starters which, in reality, become some kind of dessert: Kalix roe, the famous caviar from Norrbotten, produced by the little vendace fish, to the Child Lady. Twelve European flat oysters, or "kisses from the sea," as Sellers provocatively chose to call them as he ordered, three for each of the men. Blaise looks dumbfounded when the shells are placed in front of him, but he slurps down the first. Anna has been given five dough balls and some warm chocolate in a metal sugar bowl; she eats rapidly with the comically long dessert spoon. Sellers wins her over just as quickly. To include "the younger generation" in the conversation, he says, pointing to Anna, he wants to have an "exchange" around the whole concept of streaming, but he repeatedly says "stream-ings," something which cheerful little Anna notices. She giggles and bites her lip and waits for the Pig's and Blaise's reactions and is now completely infatuated by Sellers after just five minutes. She's sold. And as though that wasn't enough, he's now lighting up a cigarette and brazenly flaunting the smoking ban.

"There's a lot that needs streamings," he says thoughtfully, taking a deep drag. He breathes out a thick column of smoke. A girl of nine can barely have seen how cigarette smoke behaves indoors. Soft and bluish, it rises towards the ceiling.

"Don't take the smoke from the elders," says Anna.

"Listen to her!"

Sellers laughs. "*The Child Wordsmith*. I have faith in you," he says.

And would you believe it, the Maître d' has gone all abstract now: before they finish their oysters, he goes over to ask if they would like a little sparkling wine before their food: "A glass of pro-secco, perhaps, while we wait for the meal to begin? Or cham-pagne? We have the good Ruinart Brut, fresh, creamy."

Sellers is beaming, as malicious as only a scamp can be. "Fantastic," he says, "some bubbly before the meal. Thank you."

Blaise knocks back oyster number two and swallows firmly. Is he gulping? The phrase "ruddy faced" fits the Maître d' wonderfully: he's extremely ruddy, a real rud. He pours the Ruinart slowly, very slowly, a textbook example of how to pour the sparkling wine, but also straight against the traditional European serving rite. The champagne is only just running out of the neck. Like some kind of blood dumpling in a suit, he stands there pouring, well within a Maître d's custom but also verging on collapse because everything is going backwards. If it had been down to Sellers, the sparkling wine would have trickled back into the bottle from the glasses.

"There's nothing like the fizz of champagne before food, quaffed down from Marie Antoinette's teat," Sellers says ceremoniously, sipping handsomely from his shallow coupe glass.

Blaise grips his last oyster but manages to drop it and it falls, with a good spoonful of shallot and Moscatel vinegar, onto his phenomenal lapel. The mollusk rolls down Blaise's entire left flank and lands on his thigh. It leaves behind a dark trail, like a snail. It's a shock to the entire table. Everyone watching, the Bar Manager and myself included, gasps inwardly. You can actually hear the meticulousness break, not to mention Blaise's wallet jingling. Blaise looks at the Pig with an expression of disgust and then jumps up like a coiled spring. The Pig follows him. The Maître d' has frozen in a position resembling a Greek statue, but he composes himself and goes to his aid. "Let's go and see Old Pedersen in the cloakroom," he says with vigor. "Pedersen will have a solution for this;

he knows his stuff." With hurried steps, the three rush out into the foyer, where Pedersen is sitting, full of experience and old tricks.

The Child Lady turns to Anna and asks whether she isn't tired. "You're up late every evening," she says. Anna shakes her head. "You're so pretty," says the Child Lady.

Sellers's eyes suddenly freeze, and his boyish smile disappears. He points to the Child Lady with his cigarette and says, with full force, "I'll short-circuit you."

The Child Lady, otherwise a machine for envy, loses her grip and glances to one side; it's as though she has been emptied. She pauses. Anna's eyes dart back and forth. Sellers looks at me and nods firmly. And, in a rare, clear moment, I spot my chance.

"Come on, Anna," I say. Anna gets up. "Grab your bag and wait under the mezzanine. I'll be right back." Anna does as she is told; I run over to the spiral staircase and rush upwards, making the iron framework sing. Bent over at the top, I see Old Johansen sitting with his face pointing straight up and his mouth open. The back of his head is resting on his neck fat, completely still. Is he dead? No, his fingers are moving; he's playing. "What about playing one of those night tunes that Bach wrote for Count Keyserling," I say. "Possibly no. 21." Old Johansen straightens up and seamlessly transitions into one of Bach's night tunes.

Anna is standing obediently with her bag on her back. On the short wall beneath the mezzanine, that false ceiling, there is a small wooden door with a bolt. It's the old wood store—or wood chamber, if you like—no longer in use. A blue plaque screwed up between all the other adornments reads *Annar Andredagen (1942–45)*. In here, I say to Anna, undoing the bolt on the door. A man called Annar hid in here every other day during the war, they say, I tell her. Look at all the newspaper cuttings! It's empty now. Pretty good space? We'll lie you down in here, Anna, I say. Dad isn't here yet. It's late. You can look at all the cuttings on the walls here. There's a picture of Andy Panda. I have to keep working my shift. Is your bandage OK? Anna asks. Yes, it's nice and tight, I say. Thanks so much. Now let's make a nest for you in here. Come, Anna. Crawl in.

I go back to the kitchen. In the wardrobe corner, I grab an armful of waiter's jackets that aren't being used. The chef moves and makes space.

And once we've made a nest of the white waiter's jackets in the old wood store, and Anna is lying down, with her knapsack as a pillow and even a jacket on top to soften it, and we've put the candle from table nineteen in the bracket, we hear a gentle knock from outside. The door opens with a creak and Sellers peers in. He smiles. "Shall I tell you a fairy tale?" Anna nods from her lying position. Then Sellers crawls in and sits down by one side of the girl and starts.

Are you lying there, staring

What is it you're staring at
Do you want a whopping?
Control your eyeballs

Staring
Gawking
There are so many nice things to glare at

It's glowing
The glow

It's shining
The shine

Watch so your eyes don't fall out of your head
Then they fall out

The eyes roll out and over the ground
Into the troll's bag
The troll runs to the hills
Where he hammers the eyes into coins

The troll gets rich, so rich

The troll takes the eyes to the mountain
Inside are all the eyes, and they are coins

THE NAME

ANNA LIES QUIETLY IN HER NEST. AFTER TEN MINUTES she starts breathing more heavily, and a jolt passes through her body. The door to the cubbyhole creaks; I don't want to wake her. Best to sit here a bit longer. When is a child sleeping deeply? I think I should reach out in the dark and stroke her head, but I pull back. Instead, I quietly repeat her name: "Anna, Anna." I'm trying to stroke her with her own name, you could say.

Sellers has vanished. Is that Blaise I hear out in the restaurant? The wall distorts the voices; I don't know who is saying what. It's like I'm blind. Types like Blaise don't give in. Certain types like Blaise and the Pig, they don't give in. Types like Sellers, they come back. They don't give in. They're tireless. People like the Child Lady are always coming back.

"It's a paradox that life is so ordinary when it's so short and unusual," someone out there mumbles. Who was it? It couldn't be the Maître d'; his maxims are more irritable, less wondering. Maybe the Pig. He's old enough to think along those lines.

"Fame is a mask that eats into the face," someone else says. A woman. There's no way the Child Lady could have come out with something that inspired.

Anna stirs. I continue to say her name: "Anna, Anna." It's all I can think of. It's my way of rocking the crib. Her name also flows into me as I say it. It's a strong technique, I think to myself. I can feel it. I feel a weight, and I ebb away.

•

Then everything is muffled. Judging by the hum of voices, there are fewer people in the restaurant. Did I nod off? It does seem like I was out of it for a moment. I hear the sound of the General Manager M. Hill's calculating machine. The churning. She's come down to count up, like she does every evening or night. She descends the two flights of stairs wearing an exquisite blouse and with her hair soberly tied up, typically accompanied by her son, K. Hill, who is now twenty-four years old. They sit in their usual spot, at the little table for two behind the pillar. The son is learning how to cash up the old-fashioned way.

I'm all ears. I know exactly how the sequence goes. The General Manager will be given a glass of Niepoort, just like Widow Knipschild, and this glass will be accompanied by a thin cigarette, a menthol. Usually it's I who set out the glass and the ashtray, one on each side of the calculating machine, but now I'm here, in this cubbyhole, and it's getting a bit late to come crawling out. Late and strange, to say the least, to come crawling out of the wall.

The ashtray is antique, a small cast-iron hand, outstretched so that you can tap ash into its waiting palm. Stinking of cigarette butts, it's kept hidden behind one of the terra-cotta pots next to the "fat" mirror, just beyond the lavish shelves of booze the Bar Manager looks after. I hear the Bar Manager lifting down bottle after bottle now, wiping them and putting them back. Does anyone but me actually know where the General Manager's personal ashtray is kept?

M. Hill has all the till receipts from the day to the left of the calculating machine, a ledger to the right. She goes through the takings meticulously. Her polished nails tap the buttons. I hear the calculator whirr each time she adds a sum. A long strip of paper appears, the sums printed on it. All the figures are crunched. The numbers then added to the ledger. Her cigarette burns out in the ashtray; not many puffs are taken.

It's like this every night: once M. Hill sits down with the calculating machine, it's over. By then, even the slowest guests have settled up. In the cloakroom they pull on coats and jackets, cloaks. Hats are less common these days, but they do still make the occasional appearance; believe it or not, Pedersen still has to hand over the odd hat, it is put onto a head, and disappears into the night. The Maître d' remains, splitting hairs, making sure that every last thing is where it should be. Everything has to be reset. He's very particular about that last reset.

•

Anna is sleeping now, I should think. I don't move. I'll have to stay put. Through the old steam hatch above the bracket in the dark room, I can see the cinema and, beyond that, the theater, the meeting places of the past. If I move my head right up against the wall, I can also see the end section of our sign. Oddly enough, the sign is split in two, with an upper and a lower panel. It stretches from one end to the other, above the entrance, and is supported by four narrow pillars in bright orange Skyros marble. That's how it has been for years, towering crosswise like some huge European reptile. The facade has an Adolf Loos–like character, but it's definitely pre-Loos, clumsier, more provincial.

Unlike a church window, which is illuminated from the out-side, like an advertisement for the glory to come, there is an opening at the back, through the wall along the length of our sign. This means that every evening the light from the restaurant shines through the sign and onto the street. The sign functions as a kind of dim light box. Cloakroom attendant Pedersen is in charge of the two ceiling lamps which produce that effect. When he leaves for the night, he turns them off.

On the upper panel, *The Hills* is written in pale white script, surrounded by dark slabs of onyx that are divided by a flamboyant pattern of lead came; it's essentially a stained glass window, leaded glass. The lower panel is a slanted box, an oversized cabinet, with straight lines of white, blue, and red around *The Hills*. The pieces of glass here form a speckled font, with green, yellow, and pink elements. The name of the restaurant is repeated, in other words, one on top of the other; we see a duplicate, *The Hills The Hills*. Some kind of stutter, perhaps.

ACKNOWLEDGMENTS

Thanks to:

Gardar, Marie, & Lilja

Øyvind Ellenes

Ingeri Engelstad

Niclas Salomonsson

Gardar Eide Einarsson

John Kelsey

Katharine Burton

Leander Djønne

Halvor Rønning

Richard Øiestad

Peter Amdam

Tonya Madsen

Knut Faldbakken